SHOEBOX MONEY

ASSA RAYMOND BAKER

Good2Go Publishing

SHOEBOX MONEY
Written by ASSA RAYMOND BAKER
Cover Design: Davida Baldwin
Typesetter: Mychea
ISBN: 9781947340206
Copyright © 2018 Good2Go Publishing
Published 2018 by Good2Go Publishing
7311 W. Glass Lane • Laveen, AZ 85339
www.good2gopublishing.com
https://twitter.com/good2gobooks
G2G@good2gopublishing.com
www.facebook.com/good2gopublishing
www.instagram.com/good2gopublishing

FOREWORD

Lisa Johns kicked her shoes off and relaxed her feet while she paid a few bills and shopped online in the attic of her home, which also served as her office. Her wild twins were at the Next-Door Foundation's childcare center and wouldn't be home until after four o'clock, so Lisa had the house all to herself. She allowed herself to get lost on the computer. The phone began to ring, but she disregarded it, knowing it was for her sister-in-law, because no one knew she was home and most people called her on her cell during the day if they needed to reach her.

"Lisa! Lisa! Let me use your car. Mine won't start, and I'm going to be late picking up Princess from the airport."

"Go ahead! The keys are down on the kitchen table," Lisa answered, yelling downstairs without leaving the cozy plush office chair.

Only a few moments had passed before bliss was interrupted by the sound of the screen door slamming loudly.

"What did that girl forget now?" Lisa asked herself, thinking it was her sister-in-law rushing back into the house.

But a strange rumbling caught her attention. It didn't sound li[ke] her sister-in-law. But when the phone rang again and stopped, Li[sa] figured it was her, so she went back to her shopping on Amazo[n]. She wanted to get the latest book in the Harry Potter series for t[he] girls.

Lisa heard a crash followed by the sound of rushing footste[ps] coming from below. The atmosphere didn't feel right, and it mad[e] her wonder who could be down there making all the noise. Li[sa] thought maybe her husband had come home early. If this was tru[e], she wanted to get in a quickie before he ran off again. So, she got [up] and took the back stairs down to the kitchen, where she hea[rd] another rumble come from the other room.

"What are you doing in there?" she whispered, smiling as s[he] thought of a few freaky things she wanted to do with her husband [if] he was the person behind all the commotion.

Lisa's husband hadn't spent a full night at home with them [these] days. He had recently opened a new salon that took up most of h[is] time. She ventured through the house to the front second-flo[or] staircase that led up to the bedrooms. Even though Lisa's exciteme[nt] was building, she still couldn't shake the feeling that somethi[ng] wasn't right. She could feel the uneasiness deep in her bones. To the right of the stairs was the guest bedroom where her in-law was staying until the remodeling that was going on at her own home was finished.

Suddenly, she heard a loud scream followed by the sound of fighting from above. Before Lisa could react, someone came rushing out of the guest room holding a gun. She was paralyzed by fear, and the sight of her standing there obviously caught the intruder by surprise as well, by the way he yelped and jumped when he found her standing there.

Without a second thought he shot Lisa point-blank in the chest, killing her instantly. At the sound of the gunshot, another man came running down the stairs. Then the two stickup kids fled from the home emptyhanded, believing they just caught two bodies all for nothing.

SHOEBOX MONEY

ASSA RAYMOND BAKER

CHAPTER 1

"**Ms. Johns, I apologize** for the wait. Could you have a seat, please?" Dr. Scott said, closing the door behind her.

Dorothy Johns was happy to take a load off in the doctor's cool office. Even though she heard the seriousness in the good doctor's voice, she wasn't worried, because he was known to be a jokester.

"Okay, I'm sitting. What's up?"

"Dorothy, I hate to put it like this, but I have some good news and some bad for you," he explained, making his way back behind his file-cluttered desk.

She watched him pick up what she believed to be her medical file.

"He's about to tell me I have to take an early vacation from work," she thought, which was a standing joke between them.

The hardworking mother was always rushing off to work or to some kind of PTA meeting at her children's school. Normally she would deny his offer of a few days of rest and relaxation, but today she was seriously considering taking the doctor up on the offer if he made it. As tired as she had been feeling lately, a little downtime would be a blessing.

"Come on, give me the bad news," she said, grinning in anticipation of his recommendation.

The doctor didn't show her his warm, calming smile. Today his handsome face was locked in a very intense expression.

"Dorothy, your test shows that you have a very rare form of sickle-cell anemia. It's known among the medical community as Packman Disease. What this form of sickle cell does is cause your white blood cells to kill off your red ones. This is why you've been feeling fatigued lately."

"Whoa! I wasn't expecting that. Okay, so what kind of pills do I have to take for this and for how long?"

"I'm afraid it's much more serious than that. Your disease has three stages, and you're in the final stages," Dr. Scott dimly informed her. "I'm surprised you haven't been feeling much worse."

"What are you really saying to me? Come on out with it!" Dorothy demanded, with a hint of fear in her words.

"Dorothy, there's never an easy way to tell a person this, especially someone I've become fond of." He walked around the desk and stood in front of her. "Dorothy, you're dying!"

"I'm what?" she yelled, springing up out of her seat and sending the chair crashing to the floor.

A nurse and the receptionist, who were outside the office sharing photos of their children, came rushing inside when they heard the crash, just in time to catch Dorothy as she fainted.

* * *

Dorothy lived in a daze for the rest of the week. She spent most of the time worrying about her children, praying, and sometimes cussing God.

"Lord, why are you calling me home? What have I done so wrong to deserve this? Oh Father God, who's gonna take care of my babies when I'm gone? Please! I'm all they have! Almighty Father, please, please let me live!"

Soon after her prayer, she threw up blood and knew there would be no mercy for her. So that evening she pulled herself together and cooked her children a nice dinner as she tried to come up with a good way to tell them she was dying.

"Mama, this meatloaf is good!" her son praised as he reached in for his second helping.

"Ma, you look tired. I'll clean up after dinner if you want me to," her daughter offered between bites of her corn on the cob that she liked smothered in ranch dressing.

The loving mother tried her best to keep her emotions in check as she wondered how many more days like this she would have with her children.

"Mama, why you cryin'?" the children asked in unison, obviously shocked by their mother's sudden tears.

"I'm okay. You two just make me so happy. But we do have to have a serious talk after dinner. So eat up, but don't rush," she answered as she cleared away her tears with a paper towel.

They finished their meal in an awkward silence. After everything was cleaned and put away, Dorothy sat them down and told them the awful life-changing news.

"No!" her daughter, Dameka, cried, throwing her arms around her.

"How long do you got before it happens?" Domeko asked after sitting with a shocked, blank expression on his face.

"Let's not think of that right now. When the Lord says your time is up, there's nothin' in the world that can stop it!" she answered, putting on her brave face for him. "Let's just enjoy what time we have right now. Hush up them tears, baby girl. Don't cry for me. You two have to be stronger than ever now; 'cuz when I'm gone, each other is all you'll have in this world."

"But, Mama!"

"But nothing!" Dorothy interrupted him. "And I don't want you to hate or turn your backs on our God. Do you hear me?" They agreed. "He has a plan for all of us. Always put Him first. Believe in Him, and He will show you the way. Plus you'll have me for an angel, and I'll be looking over y'all always. So it don't matter how much time I have 'cuz we're gonna make do with whatever time we have left together. Now promise me you will always take care of each other?"

When they didn't answer right away, Dorothy asked them again.

"Promise!" they responded in unison, which was something they did a lot.

They all slept in the same bed that night, and it was the first time since she had gotten the news of her death sentence that she didn't cry herself to sleep. Dorothy got up and sent them off to school the following morning as always. Neither child wanted to leave her alone. Both of them were afraid their mother wouldn't be there when they returned at the end of the school day.

CHAPTER 2

Over the next few months, Dorothy's illness progressed. She ended up in the hospital for three days after she had returned to work three months ago. Now, for the past two months, Dorothy had been unable to work, and her savings and food supply were getting low fast. She couldn't gather the strength to move around on her own at times, so her son took charge, making the decision they would take turns going to school, so someone would be with her at all times to take care of her.

As Domeko walked to school, he noticed that many of the older teenage boys in his neighborhood sold and stashed drugs. He also noticed there was a whole different crew on the blocks when he returned home. For weeks he made mental notes of all the movement in the neighborhood and put together a plan.

After dinner that Wednesday, Domeko cleaned the kitchen while Dameka helped her mother get ready for bed. Once Dorothy was asleep, the children sat in the living room watching the television and finishing their homework like they promised they would.

"Meka, it's time for me to step up and be a man."

"Boy, please, you thirteen!" Dameka laughed. "What you been smoking?" she asked sarcastically.

"Whatever, punk! It ain't funny. I'm just saying that we need money, and all these bills need to be paid," he told her seriously.

"Yeah, but how do you think you're gonna do that? You ain't old enough to get a real job. So, tell me, Mr. Man, how do you plan on getting us money?"

"I'm going to sell dope, that's how," he told her in a low voice, so their mother wouldn't hear him if she just happened to wake up.

"Who do you know who's going to give you some of that stuff to sell, and what makes you think mama is gonna be cool with you doing that?"

"Mama ain't gonna know 'cuz we ain't gonna tell her. Right, Meka?" he asked, demanding her compliance.

"Okay, I won't say nothing. But you still didn't say how you gonna get it."

"Don't worry about that. Just don't say nothing to nobody, and cover for me with Mom and school."

"I promise I won't say nothin', if you promise to be careful doing that stuff."

* * *

Domeko got dressed in some dark clothes the way he had seen the bad guys do in movies. He didn't own an all-black T-shirt, so he turned his black Batman tee inside out and wore it. He remembered his promise to his sister; so, before he crept out the back door, he took a small knife from the kitchen just in case he needed to fight off one of the young hustlers on the block.

Many of the street lamps had been shot out by the thugs and dealers to help them escape the police when they rolled through the ghetto. Domeko used the darkness for cover as he nervously but quickly jogged down the alley, until he made it to the place where he had witnessed drugs being stashed. He then snuck up and stole everything he found hidden under a pile of concrete bricks next to a torched house and ran full speed back home.

Once he was safely home in his bedroom, Domeko dumped the three small plastic bags out onto his bed. Even though this was the youngster's first time seeing any type of drug up close, he knew from being around that what he had was crack, and that each of the individually packaged rocks sold for $10 each. Domeko anxiously counted 150 rocks. Doing the math, he knew he had $1,500 in crack.

He had never really seen that much money before, and he couldn't believe he had the means to make it in his hands.

Domeko was too geeked up to sleep. He sat up in bed fantasizing about all the things he could buy with the money. In fact, he had to remind himself of the reason why he did what he had done.

* * *

Dameka woke up early to fix breakfast for her mother and make sure she took her meds. After washing her face and brushing her teeth, she stopped by her brother's room to wake him up to help her in the kitchen. She found Domeko lying across his bed fully dressed but sound asleep.

"Hey, Meko? Meko! Wake up and help me in here before you go to school!" she said, shaking his leg to get him up.

"Okay! Alright! I'm up!"

He sat up on the edge of the bed still groggy from the few hours of sleep he had gotten.

"Why'd you sleep in your clothes?" she asked, before noticing the small baggies behind him on the bed. "How did you get that?"

"What?" He then looked behind him where she was pointing. "Meka, didn't I say don't worry about it? You promised, remember?"

"Yeah, yeah! I'm just asking 'cuz you didn't show me that last night, and you wasn't wearing what you got on when we went to sleep either," she said with an attitude.

"Yeah, I went out and got it after you went to sleep. I been up all night too. Meka, you should trade with me today so I can get some sleep before I gotta go out and make some more money later."

"How much is it worth?" Dameka asked, watching him scoop up the rocks and put them in a plastic baggie.

"Domeko! Dameka! Get y'all butts up. You're both going to school today!" they heard their mother call out from her bedroom door.

"Meka, go keep her from coming in here," he told his sister before he then rushed to dress in his bed clothes, so their mother wouldn't know he had been out of the house.

"What is she doing outta bed?"

"I don't know! Just don't let her come in here," Domeko said as he pushed his sister out of his room and closed the door behind her.

Dameka nervously followed the sound of her mother's voice and found her in the kitchen holding a box of Apple Jacks and two bowls in her hands.

"Mama, what are you doing? I'm gonna fix you something," she said, surprised to see Dorothy on her feet.

"No, I got it. I'm feeling good today, but I don't feel like cooking. So go get your brother so y'all can eat before y'all late for school."

"Are you sure, Mama, 'cuz I'm ahead in all my schoolwork, so I can stay home until Monday."

"Baby girl, I'm feeling real good today. Don't worry, I'll be fine. You need to be around your friends and not stuck up in this house." Dorothy placed the bowls on the kitchen table and then began to fill them with cereal. "Hey, I'm still the mama, so just do what I told you!" she snapped jokingly.

"Okay, Ma. I got Meko up already."

"You better go see if that big-head boy took his butt back to sleep."

"Okay."

Domeko met her in the living room on his way to the kitchen looking like he had just gotten out of bed. Dameka told him what their mother wanted them to do. He was still tired, but surprised to see his mother in the kitchen smiling and acting like her old self again. The three of them had breakfast at the table and talked and joked around until it was time for them to get ready for school.

CHAPTER 3

Domeko was on full alert more than usual because of the caper he had pulled off in the hood hours before. From what he could see, things were business as usual in the ghetto on this warm, humid morning.

He was glad his sister was in her own world singing one of her favorite songs that she was blasting through her headphones. They were only a few blocks away from school when Domeko spotted one of the hustlers receiving a package from someone driving a maroon Ferrari-kitted Chevy Blazer with dark tinted windows. He had seen the truck with its thundering bass zooming through the hood many times before but never stopping, which is what caught his attention.

"Meka!" he called as he tapped his sister's arm to get her attention. "Meka, keep going. I'ma catch up with you in a minute."

"Why? What you gonna do?" she asked, holding her headset in her hand and trying to see what he was looking back at.

"Just go. I gotta do something right fast."

Dameka placed her headphones around her neck and reluctantly walked on, fighting the urge to look back at her brother as he ran off through a gangway across the street from them. Domeko cut through the alley and rounded the block just behind where the truck had stopped. When he thought the coast was clear, he ran up and retrieved a purple velvet Crown Royal sack that was hidden inside a bush by the hustler. He then quickly retraced his footsteps until he caught back up to his sister.

"Boy, where did you go?" Dameka quizzed him, relieved they were together again.

"To get this!" he answered as he flashed the sack that he hid under his coat.

Domeko noticed the weight of the sack for the first time and was very curious to see what was inside. As soon as they reached the school playground, Dameka pulled him aside.

"Now, Meko, let's see what's in the bag. I hope you know I saw you take it, too. Boy, you's a fool!" she said, grinning like she did when she was told a secret.

"I hope it's some more dope, but I don't know 'cuz it's kinda heavy."

"Let's look and see! Stupid, it might be a bomb and blow us up!"

13

she urged with a more serious tone.

The siblings found a spot away from everyone on the playground and looked inside the soft purple sack. The first thing they saw were large rolls of cash.

"How much is that?"

"I don't know. You just saw me open it, didn't you? I can do it again if you missed it the first time!" he told her sarcastically.

"Forget you, punk! You didn't have to get smart!" she said with an attitude. "You better give me some, too."

"Girl, remember! I'm doing this stuff for Mom and those bills. But here!" he said as he reached in and handed her the first bill he touched—a $50.

"Wow! I can have all of this?"

"Yeah, but you gotta make it last. And don't let Mama know you got it," he warned.

"I know that already! Dang!"

Along with the large amount of cash in the sack were two .32 automatic handguns and a big chunk of dope. Domeko hid the sack in his book bag before going inside to start the school day. The day went by surprisingly fast for the two of them. They stopped at the

14

corner store for some junk food on the way home. Once they stepped inside their house, their mother was nowhere to be found.

They searched the small home as if she were hiding from them both, fearing the worst, until Dameka found the note their mother left for them on the kitchen table. It read:

Don't worry, I'm fine. I just ran to the store to pick up a few things to cook. Don't leave the house, and don't go out until your homework is done! Love, Mom.

They were relieved, so they took the time while she was gone to count up the money in the sack. The cash totaled out at $2,750. It was the most money the two had ever seen.

"Do you know how much shopping I could do with this much money if we didn't need it so bad?" Dameka stated in one long breath. "How do you plan on giving it to Mama?"

When he didn't answer her, she looked up from the stack of cash she was flipping through and saw the blank expression on his face. She knew it meant Domeko was lost in his thoughts, so she gave him some time before asking him again.

"Go in Mom's room and get some envelopes right fast," he ordered, when he finally spoke.

Dameka ran and did what she was told. When she located the envelopes and returned, Domeko had the money counted out into stacks of $500. He told Dameka to help him stuff them into five envelopes and address them to their mother. The five envelopes didn't have a return address or stamps, but he still took one and mixed it in with the mail they had gotten out of the mailbox when they got home from school.

"Here, Meka, put these somewhere she can't find them. But I want you to put one somewhere she can find it every other week, okay?"

"Yeah, okay. What you gonna do with that?" she asked as she pointed to the rest of the money.

"I'ma put it up until I can make it another $500," he answered as he placed it into a shoebox along with the guns. "I don't know how much to sell this for," he admitted while holding up the big chunk of dope.

"You know you can't ask nobody."

"I know, I know!"

"Can we just break it down into the same size of the little ones that cost $10? If we do that, then we'll know how much it is."

"Good thinking. I knew you was good for something!" Domeko playfully shoved her. "But, Sis, let me deal with this here. It can't be no 'we' with this stuff here. I need you to take care of Mom like you've been doing and learn how to pay the bills, okay?" he said seriously.

* * *

Domeko was returning from a quick trip to the corner store with a bag full of junk food when he saw a cab stop in front of his house. His mother stepped out of it and spotted him right away.

"Domeko, come grab these bags for Mama!"

He ran over to the cab's open trunk and started removing grocery bags while Dorothy paid the driver.

"Ma, you look tired! I'll get all this. You go and rest," Domeko said, handing the first set of bags to his sister, who had come out to the porch with the house phone glued to her ear.

"Okay, but don't forget my eggs and stuff on the backseat," she told him, before on second thought, she grabbed the three bags herself knowing how forgetful her son could be.

CHAPTER 4

After cooking and eating dinner as a family, Dorothy's entire body hurt. Knowing the pain would only intensify, she took her meds and then went tó right to bed. The twins waited until they were sure she was fast asleep before going in Domeko's room to start breaking down and packaging the dope.

After about an hour or so of matching each stone size for size, with the ones already in baggies, they sat down and counted the piles. Domeko put together the numbers that totaled 401 stones. He did the math, which was the equivalent of about $2,000. He added the 150 rocks from the first caper, which brought the total to over $3,500 in dope that he had to sell.

When all was done and put away, they passed time talking about school and who had a crush on whom and who was hating on whom. They discussed anything but what they both knew Domeko had to do with the dope. Before going to bed, Dameka gave her brother a tight loving hug and kiss on the cheek. She was confident he would take care of everything just like he said he would, even despite her fears for his safety.

Domeko couldn't sleep. His mind was on trying to find a good place to sell the dope without the ones he stole it from finding out. That Friday morning, he dressed for what he had to do. The boy skipped school and walked straight down 27th Street until he reached Wells Street. Domeko had only brought fifty baggies with him just in case he had to run from the police and throw them away, the way he had witnessed the D-boys do on his block. He would hate to have to do that, because his family needed the money, but he knew he could not get caught, for his family's sake.

Wells Street was a high-traffic area full of pimps, crackheads, whores, and hustlers. Domeko knew he was in the place he needed to be and didn't have any problem fitting in.

"Hey, you looking?" he shamelessly asked people as they passed by.

This was also something he picked up from the guys on his block. They didn't seem to care who they asked, so he didn't mind either.

"What can you give me for a $100?"

Not wanting to miss his first sale, Domeko nervously asked, "What you trying to get?"

"Can you do fifteen? I'm trying to make some moves, lil' buddy. You know what I'm saying?"

"Man, I just got out here, and I gotta get this money," Domeko addressed the skinny fidgety man. "But I can give you 12; and if you let your people know I'm out here, I'll look out for you!" he said like he was a pro at it.

"Hell, that'll work, and I can do that for you if you give me one off every five people I send your way?"

"Deal!" Domeko agreed, making the exchange right on the busy street.

"Say, what they call you?"

"DJ," Domeko answered, saying the first thing that popped in his head.

"Okay! Call me Cash, 'cuz that's all I'ma bring you!" he said, giving DJ a dap.

* * *

True to his word, Cash flooded DJ with paying customers. In about two hours, he was out of product, making only $390 out of the $500 worth that he started with because of all the deals he made.

"Hey, DJ, you need to hurry up and get fresh. There's always a rush around four o'clock."

"Alright, playa, I'll meet you back here in a few. When I come back out here, I ain't making all them deals unless it's for a bill or better," he told Cash, not liking the $110 loss.

Once he was back on 27th Street, Domeko walked back the way he came. He stopped at a pay phone to call home and tell his sister the good news.

"Hello?" she answered on the first ring.

"What's up! How's Moms doing?"

"Fine, she's sleeping right now. I was just sitting out on the porch thinking about you. Where you at? How's it going?"

"I'm finished with what I came out here with. I'm on my way home to get some more now."

"Don't come home. You must've forgotten that you're supposed to be at school," Dameka reminded him. "I'll meet you halfway. Just tell me how much to bring you and where to meet you."

"Okay bring me fifty and meet me on the playground at the park on Cherry, okay?"

"Alright, I'll see you in a few," Dameka confirmed before she hung up the phone.

She crept by her mother's room, being careful not to wake her on her way into Domeko's bedroom to get what he asked for. Once she had it, she looked in on Dorothy before easing out of the house and quickly making her way the five blocks to the park. When she got there, she found him sitting on a swing eating a honey bun and drinking a chocolate milk.

"I bet your greedy butt ain't got me nothing!" she yelled as he waved her over to him.

"What's up?" he asked, not hearing what she said.

"Nothing! Here!" Dameka said as she handed him the stuff in her purse. "I brought you one hundred and this!"

She pulled out one of the guns from her purse.

"Why you bring this?" he asked after quickly stuffing it in his pocket. "'Cuz I'll just feel better if you got it with you, that's all.'"

"Okay, good lookin' out!"

He could see the worry in his sister's eyes.

"I'ma call you every hour to let you know I'm alright. Here! Take the money back with you and go straight home."

"Boy, I know. I left Mama by herself anyways!"

They hugged before she jogged home, and he headed back over

to Wells Street.

* * *

By six o'clock, DJ had sold out again. This time he made $930 out of the $1,000 in dope that his sister brought him.

"Hey, Cash, man, I'ma get up with you later."

"DJ, man, I know you ain't telling me you calling it a night already, is you?"

"Yeah, it's been one! I'll see you out here in the morning."

"In the morning? How you gonna do a nigga like that?" Cash asked, shocked that Domeko wanted to leave so early. "You got the best shit out here right now. I gotta walk way down the way to get what you got."

"Man, I gotta get—!"

"You gotta get this money! It's out here. Everybody got paid and they trying to spend it with you!" Cash explained, after interrupting whatever reason DJ was about to give him for calling it a night. "Come on, lil' buddy, it's still early. Go do whatever you gotta do and come on back. I'll be right here waiting on you with a handful of greenbacks."

"Alright, man, I'll be right back," DJ promised, giving in to his hyped buddy.

This time Domeko walked all the way home so his mother wouldn't see him. It was Friday, so she wouldn't be too upset that he didn't come right home after school like he usually did. Domeko wondered what his sister had told their mother he was doing, and he remembered he forgot to call her in the last hour. When he made it to the house, he looked in on his mother as Dameka drilled him on his eventful day.

Domeko dumped the cash he had made on the bed for his sister to count and put away, while he quickly told her about Cash and how crazy the people he had served were acting. He then told her to cover for him a little while longer because he was going back out.

Dameka agreed and went back to the task of counting and dividing the cash up into stacks of $500, so they could be placed inside the envelopes. Domeko didn't feel like counting, so he just grabbed a handful of the little off-white rocks and then got on his bike and headed back.

This was the day that Domeko "DJ" Johns vowed to always do whatever he had to, to take care of himself and his sister.

Chapter 5

Early the next morning, Dorothy awoke with an intense need to get out of bed. She wasn't feeling much better than she did the day before, but her pride wouldn't allow her to just stay down. Dorothy pushed herself to her feet and then slipped into the fluffy, navy-blue cotton robe one of her coworkers had given her a year ago for her birthday.

Her first stop was her daughter's bedroom to look in on her, but Dameka wasn't in her bed. Dorothy wondered where she could be after looking over her shoulder at the open bathroom door. She moved on to her son's room, where she found both of her children curled up in the bed like two newborns. The sight brought tears of happiness and sadness to her eyes as her mind quickly flashed memories of when they were just babies.

"Let me see what bills I can put off until I can think of something to do with them," she mumbled to herself as she moved on.

Walking around the house was a chore for Dorothy. As soon as she located the mail on the dining room table, she took a seat to get off her feet.

"What's this?" Dorothy wondered after shifting through the past-due bills and coming across an envelope simply addressed *Ms. Johns.*

Inside she found $500 in crinkled cash. She thanked the Lord, while at the same time wondering who had been so kind and why they did not just give it to her in person. Dorothy didn't have any family in Milwaukee, and her boyfriend of two-and-a-half years broke up with her shortly after she told him about the doctor's summary of her illness. Although the much-needed gift was very puzzling to her, she didn't let that stop her from portioning it out across her past-due bills.

* * *

By the middle of the week, she was back in bed. She was too weak to even sit up on her own. Domeko didn't go back on Wells because he didn't want to get caught by the police or his mother. On top of that, when she told him and Dameka about the money, she also said it was more than enough to cover the bills until rent was due. Since he knew Dameka still had four cash-filled envelopes to give her and over $3,500 in cash that he had stashed in a shoebox under his bed, he knew he could afford to chill.

Dameka had gone to school, because it was his day to stay at home with their mother. The day dragged and the hyper teenager didn't have anything to do. Dorothy was asleep, and he was bored with watching TV. He went into his room, retrieved the shoebox from under his Batman-dressed bed, and dumped it out on top of it. Domeko thumbed through the cash and drugs before picking up one of the guns. He knew better than to play with a loaded gun, so he carefully placed them both back inside the box after turning it over and over in his hands. He envisioned his time hustling on the block like one of the older boys in his neighborhood. He placed everything back in the box and hastily pushed it back under the bed when he thought he heard his mother's voice.

He went to see if she needed him for anything, only to find her still sound asleep, so Domeko went and sat out on the porch to observe the dope boys making some of the same moves he had made over a week ago with their product.

He didn't feel an ounce of guilt for what he had done. The youngster wondered how long it would take for him to be able to buy all the cars, clothes, and jewelry they had. In the midst of his daydream, a clean, fully customized Buick Park Avenue came cruising down the block blasting "Money & Power" by the hot rap group UGK.

"That's me right there!" he shouted. "But only better!" he promised himself.

All the activity on the block had Domeko fraught with anxiety, so after checking on his mother, he decided to take a short walk around the block. His neighborhood was always hyped. The first thing he saw was two guys slap-boxing in the middle of the street with a small group of onlookers cheering them on.

"DJ! DJ!" the driver of a powder-gray Delta 88 with skinny gold rims called out while slowing down next to him. "Is you working?" the man asked him as he was getting out of the car.

Domeko knew from his demeanor that he wasn't a smoker when he turned to walk away.

"Then you owe me some money, don't you?"

Domeko stopped in his tracks and faced the man.

"Nigga, I don't owe you shit. I don't even know you, player!"

"Oh, but you know me enough to steal my shit! So now if you give me my paper, I might not beat your lil' bitch ass!" he snapped.

The passenger got out and sat on the hood of the car with his arms folded across his chest and grinned at the young boy. Domeko recognized the passenger from always seeing him around the hood, but he couldn't remember his name. The driver then moved toward Domeko with his fist ready to swing, but before he could, DJ drew his gun on him.

"Hold up, nigga!" he yelled while aiming the weapon.

"So you got my gun, too, I see," the aggressor said, stopping in his tracks.

His friend sitting on the car just sat there shaking his head and laughing.

"Hey, just leave shorty alone!"

"Fuck that! I'm gonna beat this nigga's ass like his mama should be doing."

"Don't talk about my mama!" DJ warned him, tightening his grip on the trigger.

"What? Nigga, you don't know how to use that. So give it here 'cuz it's not a toy. Then I'ma beat that ass!" He held out his hand to DJ. "You don't pull a gun unless you gonna use it."

When DJ didn't obey, the driver snapped.

"Bitch, I'm Mike muthafuckin' G! I run this shit over here!"

With that said, he rushed at him, which forced DJ to pull the trigger twice.

Pop! Pop!

The small gun blasted, and Mike G's body fell hard to the ground. DJ quickly turned it on the other guy who had jumped to his feet but didn't advance. He just stood there with a smirk on his face.

"Hey, we cool. I'll take care of this. You just go home to your mama and sister and stay in the house. Don't say shit. Just get outta here."

That's when DJ noticed the gun in the guy's hand for the first time.

"He could've shot me," DJ thought, running like hell away from the scene.

As he rounded the corner, he heard another shot and then the sound of a car racing off.

Once inside the house, Domeko went straight into his mother's room, collapsed at the foot of the bed, and cried.

"Boy, what's wrong with you?" Domeko heard his mother ask, but he didn't know how to answer her. He was just too distraught to speak. "Come here!" Dorothy called to her son with open arms.

She knew from the look in his eyes that whatever was bothering him was bad. Holding him tight, she asked Domeko what he had done, while at the same time noticing the gun in his hand. His mother then said a silent prayer.

"Stop crying, Domeko, and tell me what you went and done," she demanded.

Domeko did as he was told and explained to his mother everything that led up to the shooting. When he was done, Dorothy told him to pick up his head. Sitting face to face with her son, she asked him if he was alright.

"I've seen this same look you have in your eyes before. I know I've never told you this before, but your father was only maybe a year older than you are now when he killed a man back in Memphis. That's why we ran away and came to Milwaukee. A few years later he was killed for his share of money from a bank robbery. I still love him to this day. I know he only did what he did for us."

She blinked away tears before looking at her son again.

"I love you the same. Tell me the truth, you gave me that money to pay these bills and buy us food, didn't you?"

"Yes!" he answered softly, a bit ashamed that he caused his

mother pain.

"Speak up!"

"Yes, I gave it to you. And I got more money in my room."

"Domeko, you hear me now because I'm not gonna be here much longer, and you have to finish what you started. Tell me how you feel about that other nigga? Do you think he would try to hurt you?"

Domeko hated when she talked about her death, but he knew she was telling the truth. He took a moment to think about how the other guy acted with him.

"No. He had a gun too, but he told me to go home and said he would take care of it," he explained. "I've seen him around here before."

"Okay, but trust nobody out in them streets. Always get to know your enemy and never blow off threats. Son, if that money is so easy for you to get, then get it while you can. Your sister's gonna need you, so if you have to kill again, don't think twice. I'm not telling you that it's okay to take a life just because you can. Don't try to play God. Only do what you have to. Make sure you do something good with your money. Don't be selfish, and always work to make your good deeds outweigh your bad ones."

Dorothy took a break from her lecture and hugged her son tighter, allowing the tears she had been fighting to fall down her cheeks. Dorothy then heard the hard knocking at the front door and told her son to stay put before going to answer it.

"Who is it?" she demanded as she looked out the peephole at the strange man standing on her porch.

"Ace!" he answered before adding, "I'm looking for DJ. Tell him it's the guy from earlier."

"What do you want with my son?" she demanded when she opened the door.

Ace could see the mistrust in her eyes and assumed he had told her something about what had happened.

"It's nothing to worry about.

I just wanna see if he's okay, that's all," he tried to assure the mother.

Dorothy believed him when she saw the compassion in his eyes. She decided to let him in. Ace walked inside and found DJ standing there with his gun in his hand. Dorothy noticed it as well.

"Baby, it's okay. Put that away."

He did what he was told and slid the gun in his back pocket to keep it close just in case.

"What you want?"

"Like I told your moms, I'm just here to see how you're doing, killa, that's all," Ace answered him, holding up his hands playfully.

"Now you see that I'm straight, so now you can step on out!" he told Ace harshly.

"Hear him out first, Domeko," Dorothy said, before she turned to Ace. "What's your name again?"

"Asa, but everybody calls me Ace, ma'am."

"Okay, Asa, let's go have a seat so you can tell us what's on your mind."

Dorothy led him into the kitchen with DJ right behind them.

"This is all I have to drink," Dorothy informed Ace as she placed two sodas on the table in front of them. "Now y'all talk."

Dorothy took a seat on the opposite end of the small table so her son could handle his business.

"Lil' man, I took care of that mess you made just like I told you I would. You don't owe me nothing!" Ace added, noticing DJ's frown. "That nigga was a clown, and I didn't like him anyway."

"So why you here then?"

"DJ, I know if you took the dope, you must need the money. I guess I'm here to offer you a way to get the money you need so badly."

"I got the money I need already, so I'm straight."

"Yeah, what you gonna do when the money you got is all gone? Look, I heard good things about you from over on Wells. I know you ain't been back over there yet, so that tells me you're outta work," Ace said, studying DJ's face for anything that would hint that he was on the right track before going on.

"DJ, I like what I see in you, so I'ma do for you what nobody did for me back in the day when I was in need just like you. That was my dope you took, but don't worry, I got plenty of that shit," Ace bragged, showing the son and mother his signature one-sided smile. "Lil' man, you will have to pay me back."

"I thought you said I didn't owe you nothing?"

"No, you don't owe me for cleaning up your mess, but yeah, you do owe me for my dope and the loss of one of my niggas."

"I thought you didn't like him? That's what you just said a minute ago!" DJ reminded him, a bit confused.

"I didn't, but he was good at getting my money, so I put up with him. Now you put me in a spot doing what you did."

Domeko looked over at his mother for advice on what to do. But she just sat there leaving him to decide for himself.

"So, what do you want me to do?"

Dorothy's silence let her son know he was doing well, but she still was going to talk with him afterward.

"I want you to come work for me over on Wells since you already know your way around over there. I'll teach you all I know about the game as long as you keep it real with me the way you are now. Loyalty is gold in this game. You don't gotta answer me right now. But to show you I'm serious, here!" Ace said as he set a pager and a large roll of cash on the table in front of him.

It was the money he took off of Mike G.

"Mama, do you got something I can write with?"

Dorothy went and got a pen and paper out of one of the kitchen cabinets and gave it to him. Ace wrote down his number and the number to the pager, and then set it next to the pager and money.

"I got moves to make," he announced while standing up. He looked at Dorothy and said with a smile, "Your son got me out here working hard for my money today."

He then turned back to DJ.

"If I don't hear from you, then I know your answer is no."

"Domeko, see our friend to the door," Dorothy instructed as she shook Ace's hand.

DJ got up and did as he was told.

At the door he asked Ace, "How did you know where I live?"

Ace gave him his first lesson.

"I had you followed home from over on Wells last week. Lil' bro, in this game you gotta keep your eyes open and your ears to the street. And when you do the dirt, don't ever go straight home like you did today. Remember that!"

"Alright!"

DJ gave him a dap and then locked the door behind Ace.

"What do you think of him? Do you think you can trust him?"

"He's cool, I guess," Domeko answered his mother.

"So what are you going to do with his offer?"

"I don't know. I guess I'm gonna see what's to it when Meka gets home so she can be here with you." He then saw her nod in approval. "Ma, you should go lie back down. You look tired."

"Yeah, I am a bit."

"I love you, Mama!" he told her as she turned to leave the kitchen.

"I love you always!" Dorothy replied over her shoulder.

Now alone in the kitchen, DJ picked up the things Ace had laid on the table for him and took them into his bedroom. Sitting on the bed, he counted out the money and noticed some of the bills had blood on them. DJ added the $3,000 in blood money to the shoebox. He sat on the bed holding the gun he used to shoot Mike G in one hand and Ace's number in the other, while thinking back on the last few hours.

"It's all or nothing now. I gotta learn how to do this the right way so I can take care of us," he said aloud to himself.

* * *

In her third-hour math class, Dameka busied herself doing the assigned classwork. However, she was oblivious to the others in the room until her thoughts were interrupted by a soft tap on her shoulder.

"Hey, Dameka? I can't get question 12. Can you show me how to do it?" a cute boy named Tommy asked with a smile.

"Yeah, I'll show you."

She shyly flashed him a smile of her own that didn't go unnoticed by the boy's other admirers.

"Cee Cee, look at that bitch Dameka all up in Tommy's face."

"What, Pooh? Where?" Cee Cee asked, snapping her head in the direction of her boyfriend. "Ooh, I'ma beat that bitch ass!" she said as she broke her pencil in anger.

"Yeah, let's beat that hoe ass and show her whose nigger she's fuckin' with," Pooh whispered

"I'm in her ass after class," the angry and jealous girlfriend promised.

Neither girl paid attention to the short petite girl seated behind them. Princess couldn't help but overhear the two girls plot against the quiet girl across the room helping Tommy with his classwork.

"They don't say shit when I help him. These bitches are just some haters. Ol' girl's cool. She don't fuck with nobody. If they try to jump her, I'ma help her," Princess thought.

The bell rang a short time later signaling the end of class, so Dameka made her way to the girl's room with Cee Cee, Pooh, and Tasha, the third member of the jealous girl's clique. They all followed closely behind her. Princess was held up by the teacher for a few minutes, so she didn't see which way they went.

"Fuck!" Princess cursed to herself, upset because she didn't want them to jump the unsuspecting girl.

She didn't really know Dameka, but she had a big crush on her brother since the first day of school.

Dameka was fixing her hair in the restroom mirror when she noticed the three girls in the room step up right behind her. Dameka noticed that all of the girls had angry looks on their faces, and right away she knew something was wrong.

"Bitch! Why you tryin' to fuck with my man all smiling up in his face and shit?" Cee Cee demanded.

Dameka turned to face the bunch.

"Who you calling a bitch, and who the fuck is your man?"

"Oh wow! Now this hoe don't know who Tommy is!" Pooh instigated from her position on Dameka's right side.

"Tommy!" Dameka repeated. "I ain't thinking 'bout no fuckin' Tommy!"

"Bitch, you's a lie! I seen you all up on him smiling in his face, and you gave him your number, too," Pooh said.

"Bitch, I ain't give him my number. I was just helping him with his work. You dumb hoes need to get out my face with this bullshit!"

With that said, Cee Cee pushed her and caused Dameka to almost lose her balance, but she quickly got her feet replanted under herself. Knowing she would be jumped and stomped if she fell, Dameka also knew she had to get out of the small secluded restroom and into the hallway, so she inched her way toward the door.

"I don't wanna fight, and, Cee Cee, I don't want your man."

Dameka pulled the door open and backed out into the hall with the girls following.

"So what you trying to say? Tommy ain't good enough for you or something, hoe?" Tasha asked.

"Damn, bitch, you act like he's your fucking man or something. You must be fuckin' him, too," Dameka yelled, getting fed up with all the instigating from Cee Cee's friends.

Out in the hallway, Dameka found herself surrounded again, but this time by the growing crowd stooping to see what was going on. The kids formed an arena and started yelling things, hoping to encourage a boxing match.

"Don't talk! Just hit a bitch in the eye!"

Another yelled, "Round one!"

The first time Dameka needed her heavy keyring, she didn't have it on her. She was outnumbered and knew these girls were looking for a fight. So without another word, Dameka viciously pushed Pooh, who was the closest to her. She then swung and hit Cee Cee as hard as she could in the face with a closed fist. After seeing this, Tasha tried to rush Dameka but fell on her face.

Dameka saw that a skinny girl from math class had tripped her and then started punching Pooh in the face. The girl ran wild between the two bullies kicking and swinging. Dameka was thankful for her assistance, which allowed her to give Cee Cee the beatdown she was looking for, taunting her as she beat her silly.

"Bitch, I told you I don't want your man, didn't I? Didn't I?" Dameka asked between punching Cee Cee in the mouth.

After the brawl was broken up by the school security team, all five girls found themselves in the principal's office. Since all of them pointed the finger at the other, the wise principal suspended them all from school for the rest of the week or until a parent brought them back.

As Princess walked off the school grounds, she heard her name being called.

"Princess! Hey, Princess, hold up!" Dameka yelled as she

jogged to catch up. "Dang, girl, where you going so fast?" she asked once she did.

"Hey, Dameka, you okay?"

"I wouldn't be if it wasn't for you. Girl, I owe you a million."

"Well, I heard them bitches talking about jumping you in class for talking to ugly-ass Tommy, and I couldn't let it go down like that," Princess explained as they resumed their journey.

"Thanks again, but you know Tommy is fine," Dameka laughed while fanning herself.

"He's alright, but he don't look as good as DJ," she blushed.

"DJ? Domeko? My brother?" Dameka asked, not really shocked all that much, because he had a lot of the girls going crazy over him.

"Yeah! You just can't see it 'cuz he's your brother."

"Oh, girl, that's where you're wrong. I do see it. Calling him ugly is like me calling myself ugly, and I'm far from it."

"What are you talking about?" Princess asked, not understanding where she was going with her comment.

"Really? He's my twin. Girl, you can't tell?"

"Girl, I don't know. I don't be seeing nothing or nobody when he's around. But now I can see it. He's just a little taller than you, that's all."

"Princess, you never told me where you're going."

"Oh, I'm just going to hang out. I might go downtown to the Grand Avenue Mall or something until school's out."

"Do you wanna come by my house until then?"

"I see you caught that I'm not trying to go home early, huh?" Princess said with a smile. "Will Domeko be there?"

"He lives there, don't he, oh lovely, silly-ass girl."

"Oh yeah!" Princess laughed.

* * *

From that day forward the two girls were inseparable. Princess told Dameka about her family's darkness. She told her how her mother was on drugs and didn't give a hoot what she did at times. She told her about her father being in prison for twenty-five years, and she didn't know why because her mom wouldn't tell her, nor would her mom tell her what prison he was at. Her mother didn't want her dad to have anything to do with her.

Dameka told Princess about her father getting killed when she was a baby and about her mother's disease and how she could die any day now. Their chit-chat changed from that to how many boys they had been with. Princess admitted that she hadn't been with anybody. But that all changed the day Dorothy was called home.

CHAPTER 6

The year was 1994, and Meka and Princess sat in Meka's bedroom. Meka was talking on the phone with a guy she met on 23rd and Capital Drive when she was leaving a shoe sale at Payless. Princess was laid out on the floor studying for an upcoming social studies exam that Meka should have also been studying for with her.

"I'm about to go get a soda. Do you want one?" Princess asked as she stood up off the floor.

"Yeah, bring me a grape with some ice, please," she answered, never taking the phone away from her ear.

Princess just shook her head.

"Okay, I'ma look in on Mama, too."

"Alright. Hey, tell me if she needs anything, and ask her when she wants to take her bath!" Meka called out to Princess, who was already out the door.

Princess went to the bathroom first and then stopped to peek in on Mrs. Johns. Princess felt more at ease calling Dorothy's mom Mama then she did her own, and at times she wished she was her mother.

"Mama, are you asleep?" she asked quietly while pushing open the bedroom door.

"Baby? Baby, come here," Dorothy ordered weakly.

The first thing Princess noticed about her was the soft glow to her skin that was almost heavenly. Dorothy also looked weaker than Princess had remembered. She had been helping the twins take care of her almost from the first time she met her over a year ago. But what she was seeing was all new. The air in the room even felt different to her.

"Are you feeling alright, Ma?" Princess asked as she moved closer to the bed.

"I'm fine as a little bird singing its sweet song high in the treetop. I can feel the wind blowing in my face," she said as she let out a child-like giggle.

Princess didn't know what she was referring to because the fan in the room wasn't on and the room was unusually warm. It was always kept warmer than the rest of the house because Dorothy had lost so much weight lately. But the warmth Princess was feeling was different somehow. Something wasn't right. She felt it deep in her stomach.

"Are you sure? Do you want some water or something?" she asked nervously.

"Baby, I'm okay. I'm going home. Yes, I'm going home."

"Mama, you're scaring me. Stop talking like that! You're already at home. I'm gonna get Dameka for you."

Princess jogged over to the door and yelled for Meka.

"Baby, come here."

Princess did as she was asked.

"Baby, promise me you'll take care of yourself and keep Domeko outta trouble. That boy could always find a way to get dirty when I told him not to," Dorothy explained, smiling as she closed her eyes.

Now really scared, Princess ran back to the door and yelled as loud as she could for Meka.

"Meeeeeeeka, hurry! Something's wrong with Mama!"

Tears of fear began falling from her eyes.

Dropping the phone at the sound of her best friend screaming her name, Dameka came running. All she saw was Princess crying and pointing toward her mother.

"Ma?" she called as she rushed to the bedside. "Mama, wake

up!" Meka demanded, shaking her mother now with tears of her own streaming down her face.

Dorothy Ann Johns opened her eyes and spoke her last words to her daughter.

"Baby girl, you're so beautiful. I love—" she got out before she could finish and her eyes closed for the last time.

"Nooooo!" Meka cried out as she brought her mother's hand up to her cheek. "Mama, I love you too. I love you too," she told her and then kissed her hand.

Dameka broke down crying harder while hugging her mother's lifeless body.

Princess ran out of the room and paged Meko a 9-1-1. By the time he made it home, his mother was long gone. DJ showed no emotion at first. He just went right into his fix-it mode.

First, he called Cash and asked him and his wife, Anna, to come over. He explained what had happened, and Anna told him she was on her way. But DJ knew it would be faster if he went and picked her up. As much as it hurt to leave again, he had to. Once he got Anna, he was so glad she wasn't high or too high to do what was needed of her. He paid her to pretend to be their auntie when the police and ambulance came to the house. Then he called 9-1-1 and informed them that his mother had passed away in her sleep from her illness. He sat holding his sister and Princess as they cried, but he never let a single tear fall, not even when he felt his heart break. He pulled away from the girls long enough to kiss his mother's lips and tell her he loved her, before the paramedic covered her and took her out to the awaiting ambulance.

* * *

The small funeral service was held at Goldengate Cemetery on Teutonia Avenue. Ace helped them pay for everything, but he did not attend. The only family Dorothy had in Milwaukee was her children. No one came up from her hometown of Memphis, Tennessee. Some did send money, cards, and flowers, but nobody could make it, fearing they would be asked to take the twins.

Dorothy had very few friends. Dr. Scott came with his wife and said a few kind words. A few women from the post office where she worked 10 years before she got sick were also there, and they gave the twins some money that they had collected from others around the office to show love. Princess got up and sang a beautiful version of "Sadie," Dorothy's favorite song. There wasn't a dark cloud in the sky on May 5, 1994—the day the twins laid their mother to rest.

* * *

A few weeks later the state of Wisconsin awarded Anna guardianship of the twins for a year. After that, they would be eighteen and old enough to take care of themselves. Dorothy had a $100,000 life insurance policy that paid off the house and bills, leaving her children with $40,000 to divide between the two of them when they turned 21.

Princess had been spending most of her time over at the twins' house. One night she heard DJ playing the song she had sung for his mother at the funeral coming from his room. The door was slightly ajar, so she peeked in. She stood silently watching DJ holding a photo of his mother with his back to her.

"Are you okay?"

Meka was out with her boyfriend, so they were alone. When he didn't answer, Princess walked in and sat next to him on the bed and asked him again while rubbing his back.

"I miss her so much," he confessed and let tears pour down his face in a sudden storm of emotion. He didn't try to wipe them away. He just let them fall freely.

Seeing him hurting caused Princess to cry.

"It's gonna be okay." She pulled him in her arms. "Just let it out. Let it all out. You've been so strong for us, baby. Now just let it go," she told him, holding him close to her heart.

With wet eyes, DJ lifted his lips to hers and kissed her softly at first and then with more passion and hunger. This shocked her, but she didn't fight it. Princess had had so many dream of this, and tonight it was a dream coming true. She gave in, and soon he was lying on top of her starting to undress her.

"Meko! Domeko, I can't. I ain't ever did this!" she told him, fighting to control her breathing.

"I need you. Please don't tell me no. I need you so much right now," he told her while looking into her eyes.

Her sweet kiss killed his next words, and she allowed him to finish undressing her. She kissed away his tears while his thick fingers danced their way into her throbbing wetness. Princess was so lost in his touch that she couldn't get enough of it. She wanted to feel him inside of her so badly.

"I'm here for you. I'm yours! You can have me, baby," she told him after breaking their kiss.

DJ slowed and undressed himself as his R. Kelly mix tape set the mood. He took his time kissing and getting to know every part of her body. He kissed and sucked his way down her body to her creamy thighs. He then made his way back up, sucking and licking her inner thigh, only pausing to blow his warm breath on her wetness before moving on. He stared into her eyes for a moment before pushing his hardness deeper and deeper into her warmth with every stroke. Princess cried and clawed his back in both pain and pleasure as she took the next step to womanhood. Her birthday was the very next day.

Meka came home and heard a female's cries of passion mixed with the soulful sounds of R. Kelly coming from her brother's room. She wondered who he had in there, and knew she must be special for him to bring her home. They had an unspoken rule about bringing someone to the house. It was not to do it unless they both agreed on it. She moved on to her own room to take a bath and go to bed, never noticing her best friend's purse on the table.

"I love you, Domeko!" Princess admitted when they took a break from each other.

"I know you do!"

52

He kissed her once more before sitting up in the bed. "Guess what? It's your birthday! Look at the time."

She did, and a big smile spread across her pretty full lips. "It sure is, ain't it?"

"What do you wanna do for your b-day besides this?"

"I don't know. Surprise me! I know Meka is going to trip when she hears us though," she told him shyly.

DJ had always liked to see Princess blush. He wondered where his feelings for her came from. All that he could think of was how much she made him feel like he was on top of the world and how his mother would be proud of his choice to be with her.

CHAPTER 7

Later that morning, Meka was awakened by the ringing of the phone next to her bed. She lazily rolled over and answered. "Hello?"

"Ohhhh, did I wake you up?"

"Yeah, what you think after the way you put it on me last night? My pussy's still dripping."

She rolled out of the bed and took the phone into the bathroom with her while they talked. After relieving herself, she made her way into the front room where she switched on the television. As she sat down in her spot on the sofa, never taking the phone away from her ear, Meka's mouth dropped when she saw her best friend walk out of her brother's room.

"Wha—! What are you doing in there? Was that you I heard last night when I came in? Is Meko in there?" Meka asked in surprise.

Before Princess could answer, DJ walked out behind her.

"If you heard, then you know what she was doing, and why would somebody else be in my room?" he asked, laughing at his sister's shock.

He wrapped his arms around Princess from behind and kissed

her on the neck before going into the bathroom. Princess was speechless. All she could do was smile and blush.

"Wow! I see you got what you wanted for your birthday, girl!" Meka told her, forgetting about the caller on the phone in her hand.

Princess walked over and playfully threw a pillow at her before sitting down in the chair across from her.

"Hey, I'ma get in the shower because I don't wanna hear all that damn giggling," DJ yelled from the bathroom door before closing it behind him and leaving the two to talk.

As soon as he shut the door, Princess sprang up out of her seat and snatched the phone out of Meka's hand.

"Hey, you, she'll call you back!" she said, hanging up before the caller could protest.

"No, girl! You need to sit your hot ass down somewhere before you fall out! Breathe bitch, breathe!" Meka teased, tossing the pillow back at her.

Meka listened while Princess explained how things occurred between her and DJ.

"It was so good. Even better than I thought it would be. Better than you said it was!"

"Princess, I don't wanna hear no more. That's my brother you talkin' about. Ugh, y'all nasty!" Meka told her as she playfully pushed her off the couch. "So, what else do you want to do today, b-day girl?"

"I don't know. Surprise me! Right now, I'm going to see if Meko will give me some in the shower," she told her before sashaying toward the bathroom.

"Ugh, hoe, you's a little freak now!" Meka yelled after her.

She was happy for the both of them, and she knew in her heart her mother would approve of their relationship. She made plans to have a one-on-one with her brother to see just how serious he was about their friend.

* * *

DJ took his sister out and bought her a used 1989 Ford Escort from Big Bill's Used Cars so she could move around on her own. He had been giving her driving lessons here and there in his burnt-orange 1979 Cutlass he had bought months ago from Ace. Both girls went nuts over the car, jumping up and down with excitement. Meka gave him a big hug and kiss on the cheek that made him smile even more.

"Hey, how come she gets a car on my birthday?" Princess pouted, faking her jealousy.

DJ walked over and pulled her to him.

"Baby, you don't know how to drive. Remember, I tried to teach you!"

"That's not the point!" They all laughed.

"Meka, I better not catch a muthafucka in my seat. I don't care who it is. They better get in the back."

"Girl, don't even trip. It's all yours. Who else do I got to roll with?" Meka answered honestly.

"P, if you keep acting like a big baby, I ain't gonna give you what I got for you."

"Is that all you ain't gonna give me?" she asked seductively, kissing him on the neck.

"Oh please, you two are making me sick. Get a room. Somebody give me a rope so I can hang myself!" Meka said as she climbed behind the wheel of her car while shaking her head at them.

"We love you too, Meka!" they yelled behind her.

That's when Ace pulled up next to them.

"What up, man?" DJ greeted, pulling away from Princess and

walking over to Ace's car.

"Man, I need you to take a ride with me to see this nigga 'bout my money," Ace explained.

"Alright, give me a minute. It's my girl's birthday. I just gotta give her this and then we up," he answered and then returned to Princess. "I gotta go get this money, baby, so I'ma gonna get up with you later, okay? Here!" he said as he handed her a wad of cash and kissed her quickly so Ace wouldn't clown him. "Don't spend it all in one place," he warned her before he walked back to the car with Ace.

"Hey, baby girl?" Ace called out to Princess once DJ had made it back over by him. "Come here for a second."

"What's up, Ace?" she asked, now standing beside DJ again. "It's your b-day, right? Here, don't tell nobody you got this from me," he said as he handed her a bag of weed and some cash.

"Oooooh! Thanks, Ace!"

She reached through the window and hugged him.

"I know you didn't just give away one of my hugs," DJ said playfully.

"Just a little one." She smiled and then turned to leave.

58

"Hey, hey! Hold up b-day girl!" Ace stopped her. "Give this to Meka for me. I want y'all to have a good time today," he told her while handing her a wad of cash to give to Meka.

"Man, first Meko gives her a car on my birthday, and now this?" She faked pouting again. "I can't wait to see what I get on her birthday!"

Princess flashed them a smile before jogging back over to her friend.

"Don't act like that! You know she likes to shop as much as you do!" Ace told her, waving to Meka before pulling off and blasting his radio, with DJ doing the same right behind him in his Cutlass.

"Here, bitch! Ace told me to give this to you."

Princess handed her the money and the weed, because she didn't smoke as much as Meka did.

"My boo always knows when a bitch needs some cash." She smiled. "What did they give you?"

"I don't know yet." Princess counted up the money they both had given her. "I got $1,500! How much is that you got?"

"Nothing like what you got!" Meka pouted.

"Girl, please! You just got a car!" she reminded her as they both laughed.

"Let's go to Capital Court and get something to wear for tonight. I talked to my guy who works the door, and he said he would let us in the club for your birthday. But only if we dress to impress."

Princess agreed, and with that, the two raced off toward the uptown mall.

* * *

After their shopping spree and cruising through the streets, the two went home to get ready for the club. While Princess was trying on one of her outfits, she received a 9-1-1 page from her grandmother's number.

"Hey, Meka, turn that down. I think something's wrong. I just got a 9-1-1 from Granny."

"Do you want me to take you over there right fast to see what's up?"

"Yeah, maybe. But let me call back first. Throw me that phone."

Princess's grandmother informed her that her mother was in jail for prostitution and fighting with the police. She said her mother had tried to exchange sex for drugs with an undercover cop. When the officer informed her he was a cop, she tried to fight with him and yelled that he had set her up. Then her grandmother told her that her little brothers and sisters were there with her and that she had a full house, hinting that Princess should find herself some place to stay.

Princess wasn't upset by the news. In fact, she was kind of happy thinking that now her mother would pull herself together and things could go back to the way they were before she got with her stepdad and started using drugs. Princess then asked her grandmother if she could stay with Dameka since she had a full house. She promised to call her daily to let her know she was alright.

Her grandmother agreed, telling her if she needed anything to call her and that her door was always open. After the call, Princess explained what went down with her mother to Meka. She then asked her friend if she could stay with them.

"Really, bitch! We can go get all your shit now. You know you can stay. Your ass is here all the damn time anyways!" Meka told her excitedly.

"I wonder what Meko is going to say when he finds out I'm staying here with y'all."

"Shit, girl! He's gonna be happy to have his wifey here!" Meka answered with a laugh.

After going to get her things from her grandmother's, the two returned home and finished getting dressed, and then went out to the club. Just like Meka said, they didn't have any trouble getting in. They were even given a VIP pass. This had turned out to be the best birthday ever for Princess. And when DJ made it home that night, she gave herself to him all of the ways he wanted her before, telling him she would be living there with them. He was so excited to have her there, confirming the best birthday ever.

CHAPTER 8

As the hot, fun-filled summer days rolled on, DJ spent more and more time hustling in the streets. He did all he could to make sure the girls didn't want for anything, and he also made sure he called and checked in with them regularly so they would know he was alright. Princess's mother was sentenced to sixty months and was now serving her time at Taycheedah Correctional Institutional for Woman. Princess did her best to write her mother weekly and went up to visit her once a month with her grandmother and siblings. DJ also gave her $100 a month to send her mother. Princess noticed right away the good effect the prison stay was having on her mother. Her hair and skin looked healthy, just like it used to. Her mother had gained her weight back as well. Princess's only wish now was that her mother would be strong enough to keep it up and not go backward once she was free.

Meka spent her summer playing dope boys out of their money and driving the wheels off her little car. The rare times when she wasn't riding around the city with Princess by her side, she was off somewhere riding Ace. The two of them had been sneaking around with one another for over a month now, and both agreed that DJ wouldn't be trying to hear it if he knew. Besides, Ace had a wife at home. He was also twenty-two years older than Meka. Ace liked her because she carried herself like a much older woman. She made him feel much younger, and didn't trip on him having a wife. For this, he didn't mind giving her money or taking her out to eat to a few nice places every now and then. Before Meka, this was something he only did with his wife.

Meka was out with Ace one night parked under a clear, star-lit sky in the vacant parking lot of Lincoln Park in Ace's white-and-gold Ford Bronco.

"You like this dick, don't you? Tell me you like it!" Ace demanded, flipping Meka onto her back and sliding between her legs.

"I love it, baby! Yes, fuck me, daddy!" she moaned in pleasure.

"Whose pussy is this?" he asked as he pounded her tight, young wetness with all he had.

"It's yours, daddy! All yours!" Meka screamed out as she came for the second time with him deep inside of her.

Suddenly, out of the darkness, loud gunshots filled the air

raining hot lead down on the truck. Meka screamed as Ace pushed her to the floor, grabbed his gun from underneath the seat, and fired blindly out of the shattered rear window. In his rage, Ace raised his head up a bit too far and was hit in the neck after getting off two more rounds. The big slug almost took his head off. With the bit of life he had left, he climbed out of the truck firing his gun in attempt to lead his assassins away from Meka.

Fearing for her life, Meka found his other gun, chambered a round, removed the safety, and got as far down as she could without leaving herself defenseless. She then prayed nobody came to the truck for her. Moments later all the gunfire stopped and she heard tires squeal as a couple of cars raced away. She wasn't sure and was too scared to move. After several deep breaths, she got up the courage to peek out the window. After she confirmed that they were gone, the shaken girl quickly dressed and crept out of the truck. She located Ace's lifeless body and cried, sitting on the ground, half lying on his body.

The sound of approaching police sirens quickly snapped her out of her daze. Meka knew she couldn't be there when they arrived, so she hurriedly removed everything from Ace's pockets, scooped up his fallen gun, ran back to the truck, and sped off in the opposite direction of the police sirens.

Meka made it home with ease. She then moved her car out of the garage and parked the truck in its place so it would be out of sight.

"Oh my god, Dameka, what happened to you? Are you alright?" Princess asked as soon as Meka walked through the kitchen door.

She rushed over to her bloody friend with tears of fear instantly falling at the sight of her dear friend.

"It's not my blood. It's Ace's. Those punk muthafuckas killed him. They killed him right in front of me, Princess!" she told her, now crying even harder.

"What! Who? Who killed Ace?" she asked as she tried to console her friend.

Meka could no longer talk because she was much too distraught, so the two just sat on the kitchen floor in each other's arms.

* * *

"Put up or get up, nigga!"

"How you talking? It's my muthafuckin' dice!" the young thug barked back while simultaneously scooping up the two red-and-white dice before they could be taken from him.

"You fools shut up and just shoot this twenty!" DJ butted in, dropping his cash in the middle of the group.

He and his boys were shooting dice to kill time on the corner of 30th and Wells at his home away from home. It was a nice evening out, not too cool but just right. Everyone was having a good ol' time hanging out and making money. A neighbor was blasting music from a speaker that she had placed in her apartment window.

"Hey, DJ? Come here right quick, man!"

"Hold up, nigga, I'm on a roll!" he hollered back at the young boy from up the block who liked to hang around with the older guys in the hood.

"Man, DJ, I need to holla at you right now, big bro!" he insisted.

"Damn, man! Hold up, y'all. And don't nobody touch my shit! I'ma be right back."

He got up and walked over to see what was so urgent.

"What up, pimp?"

"Big bro, I've been seeing this car riding up and down the blocks I ain't ever seen before. And it looks like the nigga's watching y'all and shit."

"Alright, alright. Hey, if you see them again, hurry up and let me know. Here!" DJ said as he handed him $10.

"Good looking, DJ!"

The youngster thanked him and then ran off to scout the block for the car like he was asked to.

DJ returned to the gamble while scanning the surroundings. Once there, he told everyone to be on point for the suspicious car the boy had told him about. Many of the guys blew off the youngster's warning by stating how much he was trying to fit in, but DJ told them to be on the lookout anyway.

About ten minutes later, two unfamiliar cars came speeding down the block. Both of the cars had guys hanging out the windows spraying shots at the group of guys standing around outside. The once peaceful block quickly turned into a war zone. Everyone ran for cover, and those who had guns on them promptly returned fire as they too found cover.

DJ dove behind a parked car and returned fire, but was careful not to hit none of his own or innocents who were just trying to get out of the way. As quickly as the gunfight had started, it was over. A few of the guys ran after the cars, firing at them as they raced off down the one-way street.

"Who got hit? Is anybody hurt?" DJ asked as he rounded the corner where most of the guys were heading.

"I think Big Habit got hit," someone answered.

"I think he's dead!" another person added while running in the opposite direction.

DJ panicked and raced over to the body lying on the ground. He released a big breath that he didn't know he had been holding when he saw his friend begin to move. Habit was alive but bleeding and wounded badly.

"Get him to the hospital now!" DJ commanded the guys standing around him.

As Habit was being rushed off in one direction, DJ and the others rushed to get off the streets before the police made it there to investigate the multiple 9-1-1 calls that were made because of the shooting and the injuries. Surprisingly, the only death was a stray dog that was hit by one of the cars trying to make a clean getaway.

DJ's team was safely in the apartment on 34th and Wisconsin where they kept and prepared the re-up, and sometimes worked out of when the weather was bad. DJ sat waiting on Ace to return one of his many pages. Little did he know that call wouldn't be coming, because Ace was killed only minutes before everything went down with them.

"Hey, y'all! Check it out!" Tommy said while pointing to the nightly news playing on the TV.

The story was about the drive-by shootout that they were involved in. The news coverage informed the group that one of the cars believed to be associated with the shooting had crashed into a stoplight on State Street. The reporter said the driver appeared to have died of severe blood loss from a gunshot wound to his upper chest. The report continued to say that another unidentified black male's body was found with multiple gunshot wounds in Lincoln Park.

While everyone excitedly cheered knowing that they at least got one of the would-be assassins, DJ answered the phone and was informed by the girl who rode to the hospital with Habit that his gunshot was too bad for them to save his leg. She told DJ that Habit told her that he got hit in the leg as he pushed a little girl out of the way. The force of the bullet sent him crashing to the ground. He hit his head hard enough to knock him unconscious.

DJ told the others about Habit's condition after he ended the call. They were all glad that their friend was alive, but knew he would never be the same playful person he once was.

Once the police had cleared out of the area, DJ and his guys all went back outside on the block. They went not only because DJ told them to, but also because they needed to show whoever was behind the drive-by that things didn't stop for them. In fact, it made them hustle harder. DJ took his last deep pull off the blunt he was smoking and passed it to closest man to him, before heading back inside the apartment to check the caller ID and wondering why Ace had not called him back yet.

On the way upstairs, he received a page from Princess and rushed to call her back. She told him what she knew about his sister. After the call, DJ got up and ordered Tommy to hold things down until he returned.

"Everything alright?" Show asked after noticing the anxiety in DJ's face.

"Naw, some shit went down at my crib. I gotta run see what's to it!" he answered nonchalantly.

"Yeah! Well, I'ma go with you just in case," Show said as he downed the rest of his beer and stood to let DJ know he wasn't going to take no for an answer.

"Whatever! You drive!" DJ agreed, knowing it wasn't best to go anywhere alone after what just had happened with them tonight.

CHAPTER 9

Show talked almost nonstop as he navigated the car through the streets. While stopped at a light, he looked over and noticed DJ had not been listening to him.

"DJ? DJ!" he yelled, snapping him out of his daze.

"What's up?" he answered, adjusting himself in his seat. "My bad, man. My head is on all this bullshit!"

"Yeah, I see. Which way do I turn on Hadley?"

"Right. Make a right. It's the second house from the corner on 24th."

DJ's mind was so much on Meka and wondering why Ace had not returned his calls that he didn't realize this was the first time any of his guys had been to his home, so they didn't know the directions.

Show stopped talking and turned up the radio knowing it wasn't a good time for his boss. He soon pulled up in front of the house. Just to be safe, Show made a trip around the block cutting through the alley to make sure they weren't being followed or walking into a trap.

Back in front of the house, they both checked their guns and then climbed out of the car. DJ led the way up to the porch. He noticed blood on the handle, and his heart began to race even more than it was already. He unlocked it and eased inside with Show in tow. They found the girls seated in the kitchen dressed in long T-shirts and socks eating ice cream.

"Hey, whose blood is that on the door?" DJ asked after noticing neither of them had on any makeup, which was rare for his sister.

Even though Meka looked better on the outside, she still was a little shaken from the night's events.

"Meko, who do you got with you?"

She was unable to see Show, who was standing in the shadows of the other room behind DJ.

"Oh, so now you don't know a nigga, right?" Show joked before stepping into view.

"Show, it ain't even like that!"

She then got up and gave them both hugs. Princess did the same, only giving DJ a kiss on the side of his mouth with their embrace.

"Hey, brother, I need to talk to you in private," Meka said as she took DJ's hand and led him toward the other room.

"Whoa, if everything's cool in here, let me send Show back?"

DJ turned around and told Show to go back on the block.

"You sure you cool, self?"

"Yeah, just take my car and go back over there so them niggas won't think I'm somewhere fuckin' off like Ace is right now."

Both girls looked at DJ with dread.

"That nigga still ain't hit you back yet? That's crazy!" Show said as he turned to leave.

Princess got up and walked him out so she could lock the door behind him.

"Now tell me what the fuck is going on and whose blood is on the door," DJ demanded.

"It's Ace's!" Princess answered when Meka hesitated. "But, bae, let Dameka tell you everything without you getting mad at her. She's been through a pretty bad experience tonight."

"That makes two of us! What the fuck you do, Meka?"

"Not until you promise you won't get mad at me."

"I promise. Now tell me!"

Meka walked over and sat back down before she began.

"Ace is dead!"

"What!"

"He got shot at Lincoln Park."

"How do you know it was him? Who told you?"

"Nobody told me. We was in the parking lot when it happened."

"What do you mean *we*?" he demanded, now looking at Princess, who was shaking her head no.

"Meko, just let me finish. Me and Ace was in the back of his truck when a car pulled up behind us and started shooting at us in the truck. Ace got shot when he pushed me down outta the way. Then he got out shooting back at them, but they killed him."

Tears began to fall again as she explained the events.

"They killed him and drove away like it was nothing. When they were gone, I got all the stuff off of him, jumped back in the truck, and drove home. His truck is in the garage. I left everything in it."

"Why was you with him? Girl, you could've been killed."

"We been fuckin' around for the past few weeks. He wanted to tell you, but I thought you would be mad and begged him not to," she shyly admitted. "We wasn't all that serious. It was just sex."

"Listen, Dameka, you're my sister, not my child. I can't tell you who to fuck with or not to fuck with, but you gotta let me know shit like this so I'll know how to handle things when they come up. You understand?"

"It won't happen again," she promised as she stood back up.

"Now come here." He gave her a big hug and a kiss on the forehead. "I love you, sis!" DJ confessed, still hold holding her in his arms.

The sight of his brotherly affection toward Meka brought tears to Princess's eyes as well.

"I love you more," Meka told him, feeling safe in his arms.

DJ decided he would wait until morning to tell them what had happened to him. Right now, he just wanted to be right where he was now. It was late, and he knew they all needed to go to sleep— and he told them just that.

* * *

DJ wasn't able to sleep well, so he eased from under Princess and went out to the garage to see the Bronco for himself. The truck was ruined. It was a mess of blood, broken glass, and bullet holes. He knew he would have to do something with it right away. He wondered how Meka even made it home without being stopped by the police. DJ then decided to check Ace's stash spots in the truck and carefully climbed inside.

In the back behind the seat, right where he knew it would be, DJ found what he was looking for. There was over $30,000 in cash, some of which he had given Ace when he did his pickup in the hood.

DJ eagerly gathered everything and took it inside the house and dumped it on the kitchen table, where he sat down and tried to think of what to do next as he flipped through the cash. He soon heard his girl calling his name from the other room.

"I'm right here in the kitchen!"

"Whoa, bae! Where did all this come from?" Princess asked as soon as she walked in and saw the money.

"It was in Ace's truck."

"What? And Meka's ass didn't tell me?"

"P, I don't think she knew it was in there or she would've."

"Can I help you count it?"

He allowed her to help and used the time to tell her what had happened on the block the night before.

"Ace was supposed to be going to put it up before he got with Meka," he explained, before getting an idea.

"Go get Meka up, and y'all throw something on real fast. I need y'all to run someplace with me. Yeah, we gotta get to the stash house before somebody else finds it," he told her as he rushed in their bedroom to put up the cash and stuff he had out on the table.

The three of them piled into Meka's little car with DJ behind the wheel. He stormed it across town like speeding was legal, until he reached the Berryland projects where Ace's safe house was located.

DJ parked the car a little ways down from the house just in case it was being watched. Then all three of them got out all dressed in baseball caps and hoodies and briskly walked up to the unit. Ace's Buick was parked in the slot right behind the house, so DJ rang the doorbell first to see if anyone was inside. When he didn't get an answer, he used the key to open the door. The interior was dimly lit by a television in the corner of the living room.

"Hey, grab everything that's worth something and wipe everything down that y'all touch," he instructed as he made his way into the room where he knew the things of true value were.

DJ quickly gathered the three lockboxes and the duffel bag of kilos of cocaine.

"Bae, there ain't much of anything here!" Princess informed him as she wiped down the door of a closet she had been searching.

"That's okay. I got what's important. Let's get the fuck outta

78

here!"

DJ locked the place up, and they jogged back to Meka's car and headed home with his spoils. With his adrenalin still pumping, DJ didn't pay attention that he was speeding as he drove them home.

"Fuck!"

"What's wrong?" the girls asked in unison, breaking the silence in the car.

"The police. Y'all just act normal!" he instructed as he took his foot off the gas to slow the car down.

When he checked the rearview mirror, he saw the squad car gaining on them. DJ ran all the different scenarios through his head, knowing that getting caught with a large amount of drugs and cash wasn't an option.

"Hey, Sis, hand me that duffel from back there. I'ma jump out and run if this punk pulls us over. Y'all just don't let 'em search this car or them safes."

"But, Meko, you're driving," Princess reminded him.

"Yeah, so when I jump out, you better grab the wheel."

He caught the look on his sister's face and knew she was worried about crashing.

"Sorry, Meka! I'll buy you a new one if y'all hit something."

Right then, the squad car put on its siren right behind them. DJ pretended like he was pulling over while slightly opening the door so he could flee. Just before he was about to make his move, the car sped right passed them and made a hard right turn at the corner. The three of them all laughed and silently thanked God for the pass.

"Now, bae, drive slower, because we won't be this lucky again!" Princess warned him as she sat on her hands to stop them from shaking.

When they walked through the door of their house, the first thing they heard was Ace's cell phone and pager ringing. DJ rushed to get them, as he was curious to know who was calling. After checking the pagers, he saw that the spot on Wells was calling for its re-up and noticed that he didn't have his own pager on him. The only other numbers that DJ recognized were Ace's two other spots across town. On the cell phone's caller ID was a number that also came up a few times on the pager, only here it was titled "Home." DJ knew it was his wife, but did not answer or return the call because he didn't know how to tell her that her husband was dead. Instead, he called everybody else back and told them he would be on his way to them within an hour. He also paged Show. When he called back, DJ told him to collect the money from all of the spots.

After giving Show the info he needed to carry out his orders, DJ sent the girls out to pick up Cash. DJ needed Cash to teach him how to cook up the crack. Even though Ace had taught him how to do it in small amounts, DJ was confident in his capability to cook a kilo on his own, and Cash was the only person he trusted besides the girls to help him.

CHAPTER 10

Show stopped at a Family Dollar to buy some more baggies and baking soda after he made the rounds. Thinking ahead, he bought six boxes of baggies and some Black & Milds. As soon as he walked through the door, DJ handed him the dope that he had already bagged up and sent him right back out to drop it off to the buildings on Wells.

"Say, bae, count this up right now by itself, and let me know how much it is."

"Okay. How much is there supposed to be?" Princess asked as she accepted the bag of cash that Show had dropped off.

"I don't know. If I did, I wouldn't need you to count it, now would I?" DJ said laughing while wondering just how much he could trust Show.

He did have all of the amounts that each spot had for Ace, but that didn't mean they weren't short, nor did it mean that Show hadn't dipped in it before he made it to him. The fact that Show didn't know of Ace's murder yet gave him a little assurance that all the cash was there, because they were all loyal to Ace and knew DJ to be his right-hand man.

Meka returned with Cash and Anna right after Show pulled off. DJ explained to Cash what he needed him to do.

"What can I do to help?" Anna asked, wanting to earn her morning pick-me-up as she and Cash called it when they asked for dope on credit.

"Nothing right now, but don't trip. I got you when we're done with everything," DJ promised her before he went into his bedroom and chose the half of kilo for Cash to teach him with.

Cash's eyes lit up at the large amount of drugs.

"Yeah, boy, this what I'm talking about! D, I ain't even gonna ask you where you got all this from, but you know a nigga gonna need some cash for doing this."

"Yeah, yeah, Smokey, I know. Game is to be sold not told, right?" DJ mocked him.

"And you know it, smartass! Now how do you wanna do it—in ounces or all at once?"

"All at once, 'cuz I'm pressed for time."

"Okay, now don't blink, because ain't no do-overs," Cash told him before he went right to work teaching DJ his tricks of the trade as he mixed and cooked up the dope.

DJ watched attentively. Cash first selected a nice-sized pot and placed it on the stove. He then turned on the radio and told his apprentice that he should always have something to groove to while he worked. After joking around, Cash weighed out the half a kilo into four equal parts, and then he repeated the process with the baking soda. He commenced to mixing one of each in the pot and slowly added water. He repeated this twice more to be sure DJ understood how to do it.

"Now this last one is for you to do by yourself," Cash told him, stepping aside so DJ could cook up the last batch on his own.

Once they were done, DJ weighed up the crack after it had dried.

"Damn, Cash, you did your thang!" he praised when he found they had almost doubled the eighteen ounces he started with.

"What, you think I wasn't going to do that?"

"Hey, let me see if it's any good," Anna butted in with pipe in hand.

"No! Not in this house!" Princess snapped when she noticed DJ was going to allow Anna to smoke dope in front of them. "I know you wanna know how it is, but send her outside in the garage or something. I don't wanna see that."

"Alright, Tetee, you heard her. So you just gonna have to wait until you get home."

DJ weighed up three grams for them and paid Cash $200 before having the girls drop them back off at home.

While the girls were gone, DJ broke apart a kilo into eight equal parts that were 4.5 ounces each. He repacked six of the piles in their own baggies and put them back in his bedroom. Show had made it back in time to help him break down and bag up the crack that he and Cash had cooked into dimes. The girls then helped them count out the drugs and make sacks for the spots before going into the bedroom to finish counting the cash from the three small safes.

DJ displayed his skills for Show by cooking up the work he prepped just before Show made it back. Show promptly weighed and bagged the crack as DJ finished cooking each of the piles he had.

The girls had finished doing the math on their count of two of the boxes and were hungry, so they took a break to go out to get them something to eat.

"Hey, where y'all running off to?" DJ asked, looking up from what he was doing.

"Man, bro, a bitch needs to eat!" Meka answered, holding her stomach and putting on a pouty face.

"That's what I'm talking 'bout. Where y'all going to get food from?" Show asked while smoking a Black & Mild and knotting corners of baggies that now housed dime amounts of crack.

"Checkers," Princess told him.

"Bring us something too, and pick up some blunts," Show told Meka, peeling off two bills from the wad of cash he pulled from his pocket and handing them to her.

"And make it quick!" DJ said playfully, slapping Princess on her butt as she passed him going out the door.

"Don't even think about it!" Meka warned Show, stopping his hand in midair.

"Meka, don't be like that with that big ol' thang," he said with a smile as she walked out.

DJ decided to trust Show and told him what had happened with Ace, but he left out the part about his sister. By the time the girls returned with the food, they were finished with the dope, and by the time they all finished eating, both of the spots—Wells and Park

Lawn—were paging them for the re-up.

DJ and Show made the rounds to all the spots. DJ then had Show follow him as he drove Ace's truck to the southeast side of the city. He parked it and left the keys in it, knowing that the Mexicans in that part of town would make sure the truck was never seen again. Once that was done, he dropped off Show at his car and gave him the rest of the work they had with him before going back home.

"How much was in them?" DJ asked Princess, who he found alone in their room still counting the money.

"We ain't done yet. Meka kinda broke down on me over Ace. But there's over a $160,000 right there," she said as she pointed to the neat stacks of bills spread out across the floor.

"Damn, that's that paper right there!" he said excitedly as he sat down on the bed where she was. "Want me to help?"

"Yeah, you can. I need to go see about Meka anyway."

Princess then explained how much was being put into stacks and what the marks on the notepad meant, before she went into the other bedroom to check on her friend. Princess found Meka sitting in her mother's room. They had left it just the way Dorothy had it, because it made them feel close to her.

"Hey, girl, you okay? Domeko made it back."

Meka wiped her face. She was unable to hide her tears.

"Yeah, girl. I'll be in there in a sec. I just needed a moment to get it together."

"Do you want me to sit with you for a minute?" Princess asked, sitting down next to her. "You really cared about Ace, didn't you?"

"Yeah I cared. I told him that I loved him last night," she admitted while smiling at a memory. "But we weren't like that. It wasn't like that. It's just that it happened with me right there, and I didn't do shit to help! I had a gun."

"Meka you said he pushed you down outta the way to save you. That means he didn't want you to get hurt, and that Ace loved you too. Come on, now, let's be real, Meka. If you hadn't done just what he said, y'all both could be gone right now. I liked Ace. He was my friend too, but I'm happy you're the one here and not the other way around," Princess admitted.

After their talk, Meka went into the bathroom and washed her face before joining her brother and Princess back in their bedroom. Once they finished counting all of the money, they had over $315,000 in front of them, not including the money from the picks or the truck.

"We rich!" the girls yelled while dancing around and throwing money at each other.

DJ did join in on the excitement at first. How could he not when this was the most money he had ever seen. But he knew he would have to use it to pay the connect back so they could get some more product, and they needed to give Ace's wife something. DJ had to return what Ace had done for them when their mother passed.

DJ's excitement was short lived once all of those thoughts came to mind. He didn't even know who the connect was or how much was owed to him. Ace had never discussed that part of the game with him. DJ knew the three-and-a-half kilos remaining wouldn't last long, but he didn't know where to start looking to buy that much dope. DJ had met a few players that were holding weight while hanging with Ace. But from what he had seen, they bought it from Ace; and the ones that didn't, he didn't know if he could trust anyway because of all of the mess that had gone on lately.

"Hey, yo! Y'all hold up on all that there," he said to the girls, who were talking about how they were going to spend the money. "We gotta think ahead, y'all. I gotta keep money coming in somehow, and I can't do that if we blow all this."

"What about the other stuff you got in that bag?" his sister questioned him.

"I gotta keep shit running with that, and it's not gonna last long. I still gotta pay everybody. Niggas ain't gonna work for free. On top of that, I got bills to pay here and on those spots so niggas will have some place to work out of. So I can't let it run out and expect muthafuckas to stay loyal to me when I'm out there looking good, and spending good, and they're dirty and broke."

"So are you saying that we can't spend none of this on us?"

Princess tossed the bills she was holding in the air one last time as she asked him about it.

"Girl, I get what he's saying," Meka spoke up.

"Well, let me know, 'cuz I don't," Princess told her, putting her hands on her hips as she waited for an answer.

"He's saying he gotta spend money to make money, right?"

"Yeah!" DJ confirmed. "But I'ma give y'all a nice piece to do y'all thang with," he admitted, after seeing the frowns on their faces.

That was all they needed to hear for their smiles to reappear.

"Sorry, girl, I can't buy you that new car, but I can get you a new radio with a CD player," Princess joked.

"Bitch! What's wrong with my car? That's my baby, rust and all!" Meka joked and laughed along with her friend.

DJ gave them ten Gs each and fourteen for himself out of the money that he found in the truck. He knew school was starting at the end of the month, and the girls were going to do a lot of shopping to look their best for the first-day fashion show. Domeko wouldn't be finishing his last year of high school, because he had money to make.

CHAPTER 11

Just as DJ had predicted, all of the spots did well and were running through the product. He and Show had a sit-down with all of the workers and explained the predicament Ace's murder had left them in. They then asked their workers to have patience with the quality of the product they were giving them. DJ had been stretching the dope he had as far as he could get away with while he shopped around for someone that could fill his order for a fair price.

He was soon down to his last kilo, with his only option being to pay the high numbers he had been getting from the few players that he knew wanted him to fall off so they could move in on his territory. The girls noticed DJ was in a bad mood more and more because of the stress, so they gave him his space. DJ hadn't spent time with or even touched Princess in weeks. He unknowingly ignored her, and it really hurt her feelings.

One late night he came home to find her sitting up waiting for him with a bad attitude of her own.

"Oh, so now you wanna come home, nigga! What the fuck was you doing that you couldn't answer the phone when I called you!"

she snapped before getting up in his face.

"P, move around. I forgot my phone when I came home earlier. If you look, you'll see it's right on the charger. Why didn't you page me?"

He took off his coat and gun after pushing past Princess.

"How come you just didn't call and see if everything was okay with me?" She grabbed DJ's arm and spun him around. "I know you don't want me no more, Domeko. So just tell me, so I can be gone." She pushed him. "What do she do for you I don't?"

"Whoa, bae, where is this coming from? I'm not fuckin' around on you with nobody! And you ain't going no muthafuckin' where." He walked back up on her.

"All I've been doing is trying to keep this money coming in. That's all, and you know this. So why you tripping?"

He attempted to hug her, but she pulled away.

"So that's how you gonna act now? You don't want me touching you? I just told you the truth, so why you still mad?"

Princess took her time answering him knowing her silence would annoy him.

"How come you ain't been fuckin' me if you ain't been getting

93

it from nobody else? I know you, nigga. If you ain't been getting pussy from me, you've been getting it from somebody!"

"Bae, you all a nigga needs. You don't be on what these other hoes be on out in these streets."

"Oh, so now I'm a hoe to you, Domeko? Is that how you see me?" she inquired while trying to hit him.

"Whoa! No, no! You misunderstood what I was saying, Princess. Calm the fuck down! You know you ain't a hoe to me. I love you and want you to have my kids one day!" he told her sincerely.

This time she didn't pull away from him, allowing herself to be pulled close and kissed. As they kissed, DJ noticed his need for Princess and wondered how he ignored it before. Princess felt his hardness waken as he held her. It felt so good to her, but she wanted it inside of her. She needed him to make her feel like she was his again.

"I want you to fuck me hard, Meko. Make me know I'm still yours."

DJ was caught off guard by her aggressiveness. It was unlike her, so he decided to have some fun with it.

94

"Is that what you really want me to do? Is that what this show you put on is really all about? You trippin' because your lil' hot ass is horny?" he asked with a big grin as he kissed her again with more passion.

With her emotion flowing from her eyes, Princess undid his belt and freed his hardness from his jeans. She knelt down and guided him between her warm lips. She worked him in her mouth until his knees went weak. As he fell back on the bed, he pulled her down with him; but when Princess started to straddle him, DJ pushed her off onto the bed.

He stripped her down to her moist panties and then finished undressing with her help. DJ pushed her back down on the bed and ripped off her panties as he flipped her onto her stomach almost in one motion. He then straddled her, spreading her legs with his knees as he pushed all the way inside of her wetness. DJ fucked her fast and hard, and Princess loved every inch of it. She pushed her ass back at him, forcing him to go deeper. He had her moaning and screaming with her pussy running like a river after the rain.

At times he went so deep Princess had to bite down on a pillow because of the pleasuring pain. DJ felt her cumming for the second time, so he flipped her over, but this time, Princess took over and got on top of him reverse cowgirl style. She rode him until she felt him release inside of her, and then sped up until she was once again showering him with her juices.

Afterward they lay on the bed laughing and out of breath. They didn't notice DJ's cell phone ringing because its ringer was off, but DJ caught the glow of the screen—and so did Princess.

"Who's calling you at this time of night, and don't tell me it's the block, either."

"I don't know, so answer it and see for yourself! Make sure you tell me, 'cuz I wanna know too," he said before tossing her the phone.

"Hello?" Princess answered with her voice full of frustration.

"Is this DJ?" the deep male voice demanded.

"Who's calling?"

"If this is not DJ, then who I am is none of your business."

"Here, Meko, he won't tell me his name. He's talkin' 'bout it's none of my business. I should've hung up on his ugly ass."

"Who is this?" he demanded into the phone.

"Like I told the young lady, if this is not DJ, who I am doesn't matter to you. But if this is you, you need to confirm it now by telling me Ace's real name."

Something told DJ to do as he was asked. He didn't know many people who knew Ace's real name or to call him about him.

"His name's Travis Walker, but he liked to be called Ace because his middle name was Asa. Now who is this?"

"DJ, my friend, this is Angelo. Do you know who I am?"

This was the answer to DJ's prayers. It was Ace's connect.

"Yeah, I know who you are, but how did you get my number?"

"Our good friend, may he rest in peace, told me if anything was to happen to him that I was to call you. Since you changed numbers, I had to get your number from his wife. Look, I don't hear too well on phones, so if you want to talk more, my plane will be waiting for you at 11:00 a.m. your time. Please come alone."

"I'll be there."

"Good choice. I'll see you soon," Angelo said before ending the call.

Princess saw the big smile on DJ's face.

"What did he say that got you all happy and shit?"

"Bae, that was the connect. He wants to meet with me in the

morning at 11:00. He said his plane is gonna be waiting on me."

DJ sprung out of bed.

"If all goes well, we won't ever want for shit again!"

Princess was happy to see DJ smiling again, and she let him know it by taking him in her mouth once more.

* * *

It was DJ's first time on a plane. He was nervous at first, but it went away once they were in the air. Hours later, the small, private plane landed safely in the bright sunny state of Florida. DJ was met by a driver named Tony in a black town car that took him to meet with the boss.

They pulled onto the grounds of a big luxurious home surrounded by trees and overlooking the ocean. A pretty Latina, no older then himself, met him at the car.

"Hello Mr. DJ, my name is Cindy. If you follow me, I'll take you to see Angelo."

"Okay, lead the way!"

Cindy had one of the sexiest walks DJ had seen in a long time, and she knew it. She also didn't make following her very hard dressed in a tiny two-piece, white with clear rhinestone-studded bikini and heels. They walked down the great hall through the dining room and then a family room to a door in the back of the house.

"You have to leave any weapons you have out here," she told him while holding out her hand.

"I'm cool with that!" DJ said, not really wanting to give up his gun.

"Mr. DJ, you can't go in there with it, and I know you have something on you because of the metal detector you passed through at the door."

"Okay, but I'm still not giving it to you, so tell Angelo to come out here," he told her before he sat down in a chair not far from where he was standing.

She hesitated for a second and thought about how to handle the challenge before she vanished through the door. A short time later, she returned and informed DJ that he was approved to enter with his weapon.

The room was huge and just as exquisite as the other parts of the house they had passed through on the way in. A large Persian rug covered most of the oak wood floor. There was a baby grand Steinway off to the right of the entrance. In front of DJ were two overstuffed couches and two high-back brown leather chairs. Behind one of the chairs stood Tony, the chauffer and bodyguard, and sitting in the chair was a short muscular man that got up to greet DJ.

"DJ, my friend, good of you to come! How was your trip?" he asked as they shook hands.

"It was good. I'm glad to be here. You have a nice house."

"How's Cindy been treating you? She hasn't been giving you too much of a hard time, has she?"

"No, she's cool," DJ answered as he flashed her a quick smile.

"Now I understand you did not want to give up your weapon? I assure you that you're safe in my home. If I wanted to kill you, Tony there would have done it as soon as your ass touched the seat of my car. I have guards outside of my home that can drop a fly a mile away. I pay the very best people to look after my family," Angelo told him before he put out his hand. "So as a show of trust, please hand me your gun."

DJ didn't want to do it, but he knew it was the right thing to do, so he gave up his trusty .380. Once Angelo had it in his hand, Cindy took it and left the room.

"Would you care for anything to drink?"

"Yeah, water would be okay."

Another equally beautiful Latina came over and handed him a cold glass of ice water with a slice of lemon.

"You got some fine-ass help around here," DJ said, eyeing the second girl, who was also dressed in a skimpy bikini.

"She's my niece, my sister's daughter," Angelo told DJ. He then asked DJ about himself and Milwaukee. Angelo told him how good of a friend Ace had been to him. He also explained that he was from Sicily but didn't mess with the mafia.

Whenever DJ tried to talk about the reason he was there or asked about business, Angelo changed the subject or told him they would talk later. DJ was ready to get back home to his girl and his sister. He had never been away from them like this before.

"Is there a phone I could use? I gotta call my people and let them know I landed here safely."

The water girl handed him a phone, and after making his call, DJ asked her for her name. She told him it was Amanda.

"I know you must be tired from your trip. Amanda will show you to the guest room, so you can rest and get cleaned up. I would like to show you my club later."

DJ agreed and then followed Amanda to his room. The room was huge. Big enough to be a hotel suite, and just as nice. Inside the room he found his overnight bag as well as his gun lying on the bed. DJ picked up the gun to see if they had unloaded it. After finding it in good working order, he went looking around the room.

In the private bathroom was a Jacuzzi-style tub already filled with bubbling water. He had never been in one before, so he decided to try it out. He undressed in the other room and poured himself a drink from the wet bar, before going back and getting in the relaxing tub. The bubbling water did its job by instantly relaxing him. DJ lay there with his eyes closed for a while, and when he opened them, he found Cindy standing in the bathroom with him trying hard to look under the water.

"Can I help you with anything? Anything at all?" she asked in a sexy voice.

DJ noticed she still had on the bikini, and she smiled.

"I'm good, unless you're going to do my back for me?"

Without saying another word, she stepped into the tub with him. Cindy straddled him and reached into the bubbling water and began stroking his hardness. DJ got so caught up in the moment that he took off her top and started sucking on her nipples at the same time he fingered her warmth. Cindy moaned in pleasure as his tongue danced across her firm breasts. The sounds she was making turned him on even more. He stood up and pulled her up with him, before bending her over the tub, sliding her bikini bottom to the side, and shoving every inch of his thickness in her. She cried out louder and louder as he violently pounded in and out of her wetness.

Cindy soon started shaking from her orgasm, but she wasn't done with him yet. She turned around and dropped down on her knees and started sucking him until he released in her throat. When he was done, she thanked him and left the room. It wasn't until she was gone that DJ felt guilty for cheating on Princess for the first time. But he justified it by telling himself that what happened on this trip was all a test that he couldn't afford to fail.

He got out of the tub and dressed in the outfit he found laid out for him on the bed with a note that read: *I thought you might like this. Everything's your size. Come down to the family room when you're dressed.*

DJ dressed in the blue-and-white-striped Polo shirt, dark blue

103

jeans, and white K-Swiss. After checking himself out in the mirror, he headed downstairs and was met at the family room door by Amanda, who was dressed in a creamy pink catsuit with gold Jimmy Choo heels, along with Cindy, who was dressed in a skin-tight, black leather pantsuit and Gucci open-toe heels.

"We are taking you to Club LEX. You're going to love it there," Amanda told him excitedly.

The girls took his arms and walked him out to a red Range Rover of which Cindy climbed behind the wheel. She drove them to the club that had a line around the block. They got out and walked right past everyone and went inside. They met up with Angelo in the VIP section, where he was sitting with yet another beautiful girl. They all enjoyed the night talking and dancing. Amanda pulled out a blunt that DJ happily took to the head before passing it on.

"DJ, come with me!" Angelo told him, getting up and excusing them from the ladies.

He led DJ to the back of the club to a door that opened to stairs that led to another door. This one was a big steel door that they had to be buzzed into. Behind the door were about half a dozen people counting cash and stacking kilos. DJ was amazed at it all as he walked toward an office on the far side of the room. Inside the office sat a tall, older man who was sharply dressed in a black silk suit, with Tony standing next to the door.

"DJ, let me introduce you to Angelo. My name is Carlo," the man posing as Angelo confessed.

"Man, why you tell me you was Angelo? What's up with all the games and shit?" DJ snapped at Carlo.

"I never told you my name was Angelo. We just got to talking, and I forgot to tell you my name."

"Mr. Johns, please have a seat," the real Angelo told him. "Don't look so shocked. I know everything about the people I let into my family. But hear me, because I'm only going to say this once. Don't ever disrespect my home again by bringing a gun into it! If you ever try to cross me, I will kill you and your pretty twin sister."

"Angelo, don't ever threaten my family again, because I won't stop until I kill you if you ever touch them!" DJ promised angrily.

Angelo laughed, liking the heart the youngster displayed.

"Okay, now that we understand each other, I hope we can become friends. I have too many enemies."

"Yeah, we cool!" DJ answered as they shook hands.

"Mr. Johns, our good friend Ace died owing me for the last shipment. I like you, so I'm not going to ask you to pay this, but I have something else for you to do for me that will clear his bill. If you decide to do this for me, I will also give you an extra five kilos for yourself. So, you could leave here with twenty-five instead of the twenty you came for.

The truth was that DJ had no idea how much he was there to pick up, but he wasn't going to pass up being able to keep the cash he had at home and come up five bricks over.

"What do you want me to do?"

"Smart man!" Angelo said, patting him on the back before asking him to follow him.

He walked DJ out of the club to a gray van into which the four of them climbed. Tony took his place behind the wheel, and as soon as everyone was seated, he sped off down a dark road for a few miles before coming to a stop in front of an old farmhouse.

DJ was shocked to find Jay and Shorty beaten and tied to chairs.

"What's this?"

"Do you know these two pieces of shit?" Angelo asked.

"Yeah, I know them. They used to work for us until Ace caught them stealing."

"They are also the ones who killed our good friend, and I believe tried to kill you as well. Now I want you to kill them for the pain they've brought to my family."

With that said, Carlo handed DJ a gun. Then DJ asked the guard that was in the room with them to uncover Jay's mouth.

"DJ, man, please don't kill me. It wasn't me! On everything I love, it wasn't me!" he pleaded.

DJ wasn't in the mood for his bullshit, so he ended it with a shot to his head, quick and simple. He then moved to Shorty, this time uncovering his mouth himself with so much force that it looked like he was trying to break Shorty's neck.

"Why did y'all do it?"

"Nigga, fuck you!"

"That's how you want it?" DJ asked him, before he smacked Shorty in the face with the butt of the gun. "Well fuck you too!" he spat as he shot him twice in the face.

Angelo and Carlo had looks of pride on their faces, like when a father walks in on his son with a girl.

"Welcome to the family!" Angelo sang before he then instructed his men to clean up the mess and get rid of the bodies. "Send something home to their mothers," Angelo told them as he walked out of the house with DJ in tow.

* * *

The next day, DJ did not return home by plane. He drove a brand-new black Chevy Suburban, a gift from Angelo. It was fully loaded with heated tan leather seats, tinted windows, a six-disk CD player, and 22-inch chrome Dayton rims. Carlo drove a beat-up Chevy pickup in front of him loaded with the drugs DJ was promised. Carlo drove as far as the Wisconsin border before he pulled into a truck stop and gave DJ the product. After they agreed this would be their meeting grounds from here on out, they parted ways.

CHAPTER 12

Once he returned home, DJ told Princess and Meka all about the trip and meeting Angelo. He told them about Jay and Shorty, but made sure to leave out the parts about him and the girls who gave him the best time of his young life before he hit the highway. Amanda and Cindy took turns fucking and sucking DJ until he couldn't take any more. They then went to town on each other, giving him a show that he wouldn't soon forget. But this was a story for the boys.

The following night he called a meeting with his lieutenant and rented a motel room in which to have it. Show was the first one to arrive. He pulled up in his 1989 Impala that he had custom painted sour-apple green and sat on gold 22-inch Forged Edition rims. Habit was the next to show up in his 1993 custom Chevy full-size van sitting on 18-inch rims. The inside of the van looked better than some people's homes. The entire interior was leather and wood, even the floor. Last to show up was Tommy, who everyone could hear before they saw him. His 1982 Buick Park Avenue was custom painted gunmetal and gray. It floated on 22-inch sparkling chrome diamond-cut spokes. Tommy's system put out enough bass to make everyone's heart skip a beat.

He had Zoe, the youngster who tried to warn him the night of the drive-by, with him.

Once everyone was inside, DJ asked Tommy what Zoe was doing there.

"Man, bro, this lil nigga been putting in work in the hood. He wants to get down with the team for read, so I brought him with me to run it by you."

"Lil bro, how old are you," DJ asked Zoe.

"Fifteen, but I been taking care of myself for the longest," he explained.

"Is you sure you trying to get down with this here?" show asked.

"Big homie, you know what up with me. I've been down from day one, and I stay ready for war," Zoe answered, showing off the MAC-10 he was carrying under his hoodie.

"Alright, but you're responsible for him, Tommy," DJ said, making him a part of the team. He remembered when he was his age having the world on his shoulders with nobody to turn to, so he gave in.

DJ handed each one of the men envelopes filled with five G's cash. Everyone got one, except for Show, who he told would get one later because he had given the one he had for him to Zoe.

"Hell naw, he fucking with my money? Already he gotta go," Show snapped and then started laughing. "It all good, but "I'ma need mine tonight so I can kick it like everybody else," he told DJ.

"I said I got you," DJ said while shaking his head. "Anyway, that money is to show y'all that it's not all about me. I want us all to get paid. I know it's been hard on us for the past month or so because the work has been garbage. But I got some good shit now at a better price, so shit's gonna be better than it's ever been, especially for y'all in this room. But I gotta do some changing up to make this happen. So, Habit, I want you to handle West Lawn, since you fuck with them niggas like that. Tommy, you and your sidekick got the hood all the way over to National. I hope y'all can handle that?"

"Hell yeah, we got it!" Zoe said eagerly.

"Show, I need you to help me with the rest."

With that said, DJ concluded the meeting.

"Hold up, y'all! I know this ain't it," Tommy said, stopping everyone from leaving. "What kinda party is this without no hoes?

We back on!"

He pulled out his cell phone and called up some females he knew would be good for whatever.

"He right! Ain't no sense lettin' this room go to waste. Hell, it's paid up for the night," Habit said, pulling out a bag of weed and a blunt. "Hey, Zoe, do your part and run up the street and grab some more blunts."

The females arrived with drinks within the hour. DJ stayed and partied the night away with his team.

* * *

The next few months were good—very good. DJ bought his sister a new Mustang convertible and taught Princess how to drive Meka's old car that they kept around as a spare. Princess didn't want a car because she was always with Meka in hers.

DJ has his mother's house remodeled from the roof to the basement, where he had a wall safe installed that only him and the girls knew about.

DJ was finishing up from a busy day, when he got pulled over by the police. He had just left from serving his guy on the Eastside four and a half ounces of hard, so he didn't have any drugs on him, just his gun that he kept under his seat.

"Step out of the car, please, sir!" the eager officer told him with his hand resting on his gun.

DJ did as he was told and was quickly placed in the back of the squad car to wait while they searched his car. They easily found the gun and then placed him under arrest. DJ was taken downtown to the county jail, where he was fingerprinted and booked before being tossed in a holding cell. Once he was in the holding cell, he called his sister and come pay his bail, which was set at $1,000.

***

Meka was on the phone in her bedroom lying across the bed when she received the call.

"Hey, hold on. I got another call," she told the guy she was talking to, and then clicked over. "Hello?"

"You have a collect call from Domeko! If you wish to accept the call, press one now. If you—" Shocked that it was her brother, she quickly pressed one to accept the call, cutting off the recording before it could finish its message.

"Domeko, what happened?" she asked, just as Princess walked into the room.

"I got pulled over on 9th and Locust for nothing. They found a gun in the car, but it ain't shit. I need you to come get me."

"What happened?" Princess asked, her voice full of concern. "He's in jail?"

"What! Oh my God!"

"He said it ain't that bad, girl, calm down. We gotta go get him."

"Let me talk to him."

"Okay, hold on. He's trying to tell me how much his bail is," Meka told her panicking friend. "How much is your bail?"

"A G."

"Damn! All I got on me is like $300. I went shopping with the money you gave me today."

"How much is it?" Princess asked, ready to give up all she had to get her man home.

"It's a stack. I need $700 more to get him out."

"I got it. I got the whole thing. Now let me talk to him before the phone hangs up."

"Well, damn, bitch, here!" Meka said as she tossed Princess the phone after telling DJ they were coming to get him out.

As soon as the call ended, the girls raced out of the house. Meka let Princess post the bail since it was her money. It took the jail over two hours to release DJ, but at least he was free for now

CHAPTER 13

After months of running back and forth to court, DJ was sentenced to serve thirteen months in the house of corrections (HOC). The judge gave him three days to turn himself in to the county jail. As much as DJ wanted to run, he knew it would be best to get the little time over with so he could get back to handling his business. He set things up so the girls could make the pickups from Angelo, and he made sure Meka knew how to get to the meeting place. Princess made him spend the last day with her. DJ didn't mind it one bit, because she showered him with all the things he loved and gave herself to him in any and every way he could think.

DJ was transferred by bus to the HOC after turning himself in at the jail. As the prison bus rolled up to the compound, DJ saw that it was spread out across a large fenced-in area. The section of the prison he was taken to was made up of three parts. DJ was taken to the old building and placed in G-dorm. Each dorm housed seventy men on thirty-five bunk beds. It had a small TV room with two tables for playing games and one television.

DJ's bed was in the back of the dorm on bunk 45. The first thing he had to get used to was that it was almost always loud, and he also had to be mindful of the phone. Some days the men made the officers work hard for their money, but most of the time they stayed clear of each other. Correctional officer (CO) Anderson was one of the regular officers in G-dorm. All he ever did when he came in to work was drink his beloved coffee and read the paper. Anderson was quick to tell DJ not to fuck with him, his coffee, or his newspaper—and in that order.

The back of the dorm was where most of the inmates hung out. While some of them did pushups and dips off of the locker boxes and bunks, others would just sit around talking about things out in the world. DJ fell right in with the guys who worked out. He wanted to put on some weight and muscle to look good for his girl anyway.

One day his bunkmate, Rain, who was a tall, jet-black guy with long braids, asked him to work out with him.

"Hey, bunkie, do you wanna start working out together? The nigga I used to work out with got out last night."

DJ saw that Rain was about his age, which was nice because the rest of the guys in the dorm were older.

"Man, I don't wanna slow you down. I ain't done a pushup since

I was in middle school," he admitted.

"Well, all you got is time now, nigga. You may as well get back on your shit and start doing something."

The two of them started working out together with weights, lifting six nights a week.

In the six months before Rain was released, he helped DJ turn his soft 155 pounds into 185 pounds of ripped muscle.

* * *

Show helped Meka hold down things while her brother was gone. Even though Meka knew DJ trusted him, she never took Show along with her and Princess when they had to go meet the connect. She hadn't met him herself. Carlo would make it to the spot before they made it there and park the truck with the product in it. He would then go hide somewhere close so he could keep an eye on it without being seen.

The girls didn't mind. Meka would casually pull in next to the truck, and Princess would get out and exchange the bags, leaving the money and taking the product. Once she made it home safely, she would send a page code to Carlo to let him know. They would then issue two kilos of the product to Show when he needed it. Show did

117

all the picks from the spots and gave Meka the cash with no trouble. Show had a thing for Meka and made sure she knew it every chance he could. One Saturday afternoon while Princess was away visiting DJ, Show called Meka to re-up and drop off the money from the night before.

"I need to see you. I'ma be there in a minute, so be ready."

"Baby, I'm always ready for you."

"Yeah? I'ma see about that when I get there. I'ma make you stop playing with me. When I hit that one good time, your ass is mine."

"Boy, please!" she laughed sarcastically. "I'm at the house, so come on in!"

When Show made it to her house, Meka opened the door for him dressed in an oversized sunflower T-shirt and no panties. She was teasing him. She liked to mess with his head for the fun of it. Show wasn't a bad-looking man. He stood six foot two, weighed about two hundred pounds, and had skin so dark it shined. He kept his head shaved and always wore a two-carat diamond in his ear. Show was always dressed nicely in the latest styles. Today she noticed he was wearing an Enyce outfit. It was white and blue. The jacket was red and white, and his shirt was white with red-and-blue lettering. He finished it off with faded jeans and a pair of red, white, and blue Nike Airforce Ones. He also had on his ninety-carat diamond necklace that read Showboy in rose gold.

"I see you looking good in your shirt and panties," he flirted after handing her the bag of cash as he walked into the house.

"How do you know I got on panties?" she flirted back, closing the door behind him.

Show turned to get a better look, wondering if she did or didn't. He liked the way the shirt just barely covered her plump booty.

Show liked her medium height, full breasts, slim hips, and long, toned legs. Meka had a round face, brown eyes, sexy full lips, short light brown hair, and skin the color of the sweetest honey.

"I need to cook something up right quick. Can I do it here to save me some time?" he asked, already breaking open one of the bricks.

"Yeah, go 'head. You want me to help?"

"What you know about whipping up this work?"

"Nigga, you must've forgot who my brotha is. I'ma bad bitch. I'll bring all that shit back and then some, like pow," she told him while bending over to fetch DJ's cooking utensils from the cabinet beneath the kitchen sink.

"Oh, damn, girl! You don't got no panties on for real!" Show voiced his surprise.

Meka really had forgotten that she wasn't wearing any, but was a bit ashamed that he saw her goods. It kind of turned her and made her moist after he said something. Meka was already listening to Jaheim's *Ghetto Classics* CD when his strong soulful voice began to sing his hit single titled "Anything."

"Didn't I tell you that you was gonna stop playing with me?" Show asked.

"Yeah, you said it. Now what you gonna do about it?" she dared him, standing up close to him with her hand on her hip.

Show closed the space that was left between them and scooped her up off her feet like she was a feather. He set her on the table, parted her legs, got down on his knee, and shoved his head between her thighs. He flicked his skillful tongue over her clit and sucked it just hard enough to make her pull her own hair. It excited him to hear Meka's moans and to feel her soft hands on his head as she tried to grind out her orgasm. Show didn't come up until she was done cumming. When he did, he wiped his face with her shirt and stood there smiling as she tried to catch her breath.

"I told you what I was gonna do to you, didn't I?" he teased chuckling.

She smiled as she hopped off the table.

"Boy, you must think I'm a punk."

Meka then reached down, undid his jeans, and began stroking his hardness. She sucked on his bottom lip as they kissed, before she dropped to her knees and twirled her tongue around his tip a few times before taking him in her warm mouth until it touch her throat. Meka licked and sucked his hardness like it was her favorite lollipop, until she felt him about to bust. She pulled away just in time, allowing him to release all over her shirt.

"Now, let me go get cleaned up so we can get this work done," she told him as she stood up and walked toward the bathroom. "And you still ain't hit this pussy, punk!" she yelled, before she closed the bathroom door on him before he tried to come inside with her—even though Meka wouldn't have stopped him if he had tried.

* * *

After having a nice visit with his girl and sister for his birthday, DJ returned to the dorm to find someone sitting on his bed talking with another guy who was sitting on the empty bunk next to his.

"Say, pimp, you wanna get off my bed?"

"Oh, this you? Fuck you, nigga! I'm talking, so go do something for a second!" Boss told him as he went back to what he was saying.

"Fuck you, nigga! Get the fuck off my shit!" DJ snapped, stepping between the bunks with the two ready for action.

"Whoa, now, G! Alright, gangsta, ain't no need to call the police," Boss said as he stood up. "Yeah, nigga, you need to learn some respect. Ain't no guns in here, remember that!"

"Whatever nigga, just move around!" DJ told him as he and his guy pushed passed him to get out from between the bunks.

He watched them head to the other side of the dorm.

An hour later, CO Anderson announced rec and then released the dorm to get down to the gym. DJ was the last to leave because he was on the phone with Princess. When he made it to the bottom of the dimly lit staircase, he was jumped from behind by someone big and strong. DJ felt the man's power as his arm tightened around his neck, while at the same time yanking DJ up off his feet with the chokehold. DJ fought the best he could, trying to break loose as he felt the hold slowing the air to his lungs. Boss suddenly stepped into view and hit DJ twice in the face, fast and hard.

"I told you I was gonna teach you some respect, bitch-ass

nigga!" Boss barked, punching him once more before stepping aside so another guy could get in a few licks.

The next man beat DJ's ribs up with a broomstick before he turned the punishment back over to Boss, who outweighed DJ by a good hundred pounds. If DJ did get loose, he still wouldn't be a match for the three of them. Boss gave DJ a devastating blow to the stomach that made him buckle, and the guy holding him let him fall to the cold, hard floor. The beating didn't stop there. All three of them kicked and stomped DJ as he lay helpless while trying to cover his head from angry feet. As fast as the beating started, it stopped when they heard footsteps coming down the steps. The three ran away before CO Anderson made it down.

"Muthafucka!" he yelled, dropping his coffee and calling for help at the sight of DJ's bloody and beaten body lying on the floor.

A flood of officers came running along with a few nurses. DJ was taken to the medical unit to be examined. He was surprised to find out he did not suffer from any broken bones, because of the way his body hurt. DJ took the beating like a man and didn't tell them who did it. DJ had other plans for Boss and his crew. Since he wouldn't tell on them, he was moved off the dorm to the Annex building for his safety and the safety of the ones behind the beating.

The Annex was a whole different setup from the old building. The dorms were a little smaller and only housed fifty inmates, but the bathrooms were bigger than in the old building. But unlike the old building, the shower area had a big window through which the officers could see from their desk and as they made rounds.

The dorm DJ was placed in had all female officers working in it. Working the first shift was a white woman with dyed red hair named Ms. Smitt, who was maybe around forty. On the second shift was an Asian woman whose age was hard to tell, but she had a medium build and her name was May Li. On third shift was a black woman who reminded everyone of the singer Fantasia. She wore her hair in the same short wrap and everything. Her name was Lisa King. She was in her mid-twenties and very attractive. Ms. King was the talk of the dorm. There wasn't a name in there that didn't wish to know her better. But she was always by the book, and only said what needed to be said when an inmate talked to her. She spent most of her shift reading or studying her school books. But every once in awhile one of her fellow officers would stop in to keep her company.

Because of the beating DJ was giving, he no longer slept soundly, and he spent most of his nights reading in the dimly lit dorm. This gave him time to see all that went on around him at night.

124

CHAPTER 14

Meka took her brother's advice and did it up for their birthday. She and Princess hit up Club Questions on Saturday night, and both were dressed to impress. Meka wore a multi-colored, blue-fitted dress by Do U Couture, heels by Cesare Paciotti, and jewelry by J. Lo to make her shine just right. Princess looked just as hot wearing a blood-red blouse, a black skin-tight skirt, and red peep-toe studded heels all by Bebe. She topped it off with jewelry by Pink Paisley.

The whole city seemed to have come out for Meka's twenty-second birthday party, and the girls made sure to party hard with them. Princess wasn't much of a drinker, so it didn't take much to get her lit. But she did like to smoke, and she got higher than an airplane off of all of the blunts that were passed her way throughout the night.

"Hey, Princess, you gotta drive my car home because I'm going to the telly to get my brains fucked out by D-town and Rio."

"Girl, both at the same time?" Princess asked, expressing her surprise. "You's a little hoe tonight, ain't you?"

"And you know it!" Meka answered, laughing at her friend's

expression. "I'm twenty-two now, and my twin ain't here to party with me, so I'ma have some stupid fun tonight. Yeah, I may hate myself in the morning, but I'ma love it right now."

Princess shook her head knowing she wasn't going to talk Meka out of what she was going to do.

"Girl, call me and let me know where you at and what room you in just in case. I need to see what kinda car they driving, too."

"Okay, mom," Meka joked, but agreed to her friend's terms, knowing she was only trying to look out for her. "The photo booth is up. I'ma get them to take a picture with us."

"No, I don't wanna be in no pictures with them. What if Meko sees it and thinks I was out being a hoe like yo ass?"

"Princess, you don't gotta take it with them, just me. I'ma take one with them so you can have it just in case, like you said. So come on."

Meka pulled her by her hand over to where the guys were standing and waiting for her.

Right after taking the photos, the four of them walked out of the loud, smoky club. In the parking lot, Princess made a mental note of the white-and-light-blue Chrysler LHS Meka had gotten into with the guys. The girls exchanged air kisses before going their separate ways. D-town received a call that made him have to break up the trio.

After dropping him off, Meka had Rio stop at a Walgreens that was on the way to the motel. She picked up a few things to make sure she still had a safe and fun night. Meka glanced over at her date and wished it was Show she was with. She knew he would've come running had she called, but she didn't want him to know just how much she was really into him in case he didn't feel the same way.

In the room, Rio leaned down to kiss Meka's lips. Instead, she gave him her cheek, but did not hesitate pressing herself against his tall frame.

"Hmmmmm, I think this muthafucka wanna come out to play!" she purred, rubbing her warm body against his hard thickness before quickly dropping his jeans and squeezing his hardness in her hand.

"Take your clothes off!"

He didn't question her. He just peeled off everything, dropping his clothes onto the floor right where he stood. Meka slipped out of her heels but made no effort to remove her dress. She ordered him to lie down on the bed as she went into her bag of goodies and removed a small bottle of Stay Hard, an erection-stimulating massage oil, and a pack of condoms.

"Do you trust me?" Meka asked while getting in bed next to him and taking hold of his already fully erect hardness.

"It depends on what you got in mind," he answered, loving the way her hands felt as she massaged the oil on him before she slipped on the condom.

"I got all night in mind, and this here will make that happen for me. You do want me happy for my birthday, right?"

"Do your thang, girl!"

Rio didn't care what she did at this point as long as he got deep into her wetness.

Meka climbed on top of his hardness and slowly twirled herself down his thickness with her dress pulled up around her waist. She rode him nice and slow, allowing him to feel her cumming as she went. As the sensation built, so did her pace. Meka tossed her head back as she slammed him in and out of her over and over. Rio slowed her down by removing her dress so he could play with her nipples. She leaned over and buried Rio's face between her breasts, and he eagerly sucked her hard nipples between his lips. The two moaned and sexed the night away. Unknown to Rio, Meka was fantasizing about doing all she was doing with him to Show.

* * *

Princess drove straight home, rushing into the house to use the bathroom. She never noticed the shadowy guy standing across the street watching the house as she staggered inside. After relieving herself, she prepared a hot bubble bath before going into her bedroom where she stripped down to her lingerie. Princess was heading back into the bathroom when she discovered she had left the door ajar. She walked over to close and lock it, when suddenly it struck her hard in the face and knocked the wind out of her. Princess was slightly dazed by the blow when she saw the intruder materialize through the doorway. He punched her hard enough to send her crashing to the floor before he then pounced on top of her. Princess tried to fight him off, but he was too wild and strong for her. She could smell his sweat and beer on his breath as he continued to beat her, knocking the fight right out of her. The last thing Princess felt was pain as he forced himself inside her.

* * *

Meka was up and out of the hotel room before sunrise, leaving her date asleep in bed. Not wanting to wake Princess, she took a cab to the house. Once she arrived home, the first thing that caught Meka's attention was the sloppy parking job Princess had done. She shook her head and paid the driver before briskly walking up to the porch.

Meka found the door ajar, and when she stepped inside, she found her friend lying on the floor in a puddle of blood with her face badly beaten. Meka screamed at the sight of her friend. Her first thought was that Princess was dead, but then she noticed her chest moving, so she knew Princess was just unconscious. Meka called 9-1-1 as fast as she could.

"9-1-1! What's your emergency?"

"I need help! My friend! I came home, and she is all covered in blood on the floor!"

"Okay, ma'am, help is on the way. Can you tell me if she's alive?"

"Yeah, I see her breathing. Please hurry!"

Meka sat down on the floor with Princess's head resting in her lap until the ambulance and police arrived at the house.

The police agreed to allow her to ride to the hospital in the ambulance with Princess, after making sure she wasn't the threat.

Once at the county hospital, Meka was ushered into one of the family waiting rooms so the doctors could do what they could for Princess. Meka paced and sat in the waiting room shaking with anger and worry. She wondered who could have done this to Princess, and she blamed herself for leaving her alone last night. Meka knew whoever attracted Princess had to have followed her home from somewhere she had stopped on her way home from the club, because she watched Princess pull away from Questions at the same time she did.

A few hours later the doctor came in and informed Meka that Princess was going to be fine, but they were not able to save the baby. Meka didn't know Princess was pregnant, but still broke down crying for the unborn child. They allowed her to sit in the room with Princess. It was there she decided not to tell her brother about the rape or the loss of the baby while he was in jail. Meka planned to just tell him that Princess was in the hospital for whatever came to her mind if he called. She knew it was best that Princess told him herself about the child when she felt the time was right. As for the rape, Meka needed to know as much as she could so she and Show could handle it.

CHAPTER 15

Princess was held in the hospital for two days. When she got back home, she wasn't the same lively person she once was. She didn't eat or sleep much. Meka knew her depression was really bad when Princess wouldn't accept any of DJ's calls. A few days later, she came home from picking them up something to eat to find Princess packing her things.

"Princess, what's going on? Where you going?"

"I don't know. I just need to get away. I can't stay in this house anymore. I can see his face and still smell him when I close my eyes. I-I just gotta get away from everything for awhile!" Princess explained while stuffing clothing in one of DJ's oversized duffel bags.

"Okay, but where you gonna go? If you want, I'll get us a hotel room and we can stay there until Domeko comes home."

"No! I'm going to my grandmother's house. I need to be around them. Meka, I don't think I can stay in this city knowing that punk is out there somewhere," she confessed.

That day that Princess left, she moved all the way to Atlanta with the family she had living down there. She planned on never returning to Milwaukee again. The hardest part of her move was leaving DJ behind. Princess loved him very much but couldn't bear to see his face after what had happened to her and their unborn child. Princess planned to call him one day and explain, but not until she got herself back together. She just needed to heal inside and out before she faced any of them again.

Meka had no other choice but to tell DJ that Princess had moved away. She still couldn't bring herself to tell him the truth, but after she witnessed the way DJ reacted to the news of Princess leaving, Meka knew she had made the right choice.

DJ's poor heart was crushed. He knew his being locked up was hard on her, but she assured him she could handle it as long as they talked every day and she could visit him. To him, her move was crazy because they were doing so well and he only had a few months to go. The only thing that made sense to him was telling himself that Princess had found someone else. DJ used these thoughts to push his first love out of his heart the best he could. He began working out even harder as his way of dealing with the pain of his heart.

Taking a shower after his intense nightly workout, he caught CO

King's eyes lingering on him longer than they should have. DJ continued to shower turning toward her. He locked eyes with her as he teasingly soaped and washed himself. She gave him a sexy smile and licked her lips as she got up to make her rounds of the dorm.

DJ didn't take their exchange as more than just having fun. After the shower, he sat up in his bunk reading the newspaper.

"What was all that about in the shower, mister?"

"I don't know what you're talking about. I was just taking a shower, but I was wondering the same thing about you," he answered, looking up into the face of her sexy voice.

"Well, since you don't know, don't let it happen again," she playfully scolded him, smiling the whole time.

"Is that what you really want, 'cuz I think you need something more, and I'm just the person you need to give it to you, sexy," DJ flirted back.

From that night on, Lisa would flirt with DJ and he would do the same every time she worked. They were careful not to allow the others in the dorm catch them, even though the vibe between them was so strong that it made it hard to breathe when they were close to one another.

One late night when everyone was asleep in the dorm, DJ thought he would try his luck. He told her to unlock the store room before she made her rounds. Lisa did as he asked, nervously knowing what she had fantasized about happening just that morning was about to come true. Just as she had dreamt it, DJ was waiting in the store room when she returned. After giving the dorm a quick nervous scan, she joined him and closed the door behind her.

DJ pulled her toward him and kissed her deeply, with her lustfully returning it and willingly giving in to him. Before long, DJ had Lisa bent over some boxes pounding her nice and hard, just the way she needed him to.

"This what you been begging for, ain't it?" he asked repeatedly in the beginning after each powerful thrust he gave her.

"Yes, yes! Boy, you gonna make me scream!" she mumbled while fighting her desire to get loud.

DJ felt her body tensing up and knew she was about to cum.

"No, no, no! I want to see your face as you cum for me," he told her, pulling out of her wetness.

Lisa turned around and stepped out of one of her pants legs so she could spread her legs wider for him. This time she pulled DJ into her for a kiss as he slid easily back inside of her, filling her all the way up again and again until they came almost together.

Afterward, they eased back out of the room and Lisa quickly excused herself to go clean herself up. When she got back, DJ sat up talking to her until the sun came up. The connection between them was still just as strong. Lisa felt a little sad that she had the next three days off from work.

It seemed like Lisa thought of Domeko Johns every second until she could return to work and see him. She cursed herself for not leaving him her phone number before she took off, but that night she wasn't thinking straight. Neither of them were.

When Lisa did return to work, she found out that DJ wasn't there any longer. He had gotten lucky and was released two months early due to overcrowding and his good behavior. Lisa was broken-hearted, and she felt that what they had was more than just sex. What Lisa felt was a true connection of heart and soul with him.

Lisa was in a bad mood her entire shift, and she took it out on the inmates by closing the dayroom early. She even wrote a few tickets for petty things she would usually look over. Lisa even considered taking her chances asking the records clerk for DJ's information. She knew it was frowned upon to get personal with an inmate. They even had what they called the Wall of Shame—a wall of photos of officers and the inmates with whom they got mixed up. This was not something Lisa wanted on her record, so she dropped the idea of talking to records. All she could do was hope their paths would cross again outside of the HOC.

At the end of her shift, Lisa rushed to get away from there. When she climbed into her car to head home, she found a single, long-stemmed pink rose and a cell phone lying on the passenger seat. Lisa picked up the rose as she scanned the parking lot of cars around her for who could have placed the things in her locked car. But she knew the answer. It was Domeko Johns. She then read the card attached to the rose:

I bet you thought you got away from me, didn't you? No, Lisa, I promised to give you what you needed, and that's just what I intend to do. So if you're feeling the way I'm feeling, all you gotta do is pick up the cell and press 1 to bless me with your angelic voice. Truly yours, DJ.

Lisa was so happy that she screamed and hit her head dancing around in her car seat. After that call, they were the couple she knew they were meant to be from the start.

* * *

Two years later, Lisa gave birth to twin girls, making both DJ and his sister the happiest they had been in a long time. A year after the girls were born, DJ and Lisa got married. Lisa was three years older than DJ, but you couldn't tell from looking at him because the streets had long hardened his face.

DJ purchased an old English home for them in Wauwatosa, Wisconsin, with five bedrooms, two-and-a-half bathrooms, and a two-car garage. DJ stepped back and allowed Lisa to furnish the place. She had custom drapes installed that opened and closed with the push of a button, a stainless-steel kitchen, polished oak hardwood floors, and black-and-tan leather furniture to complement the family room. Lisa bought everything she liked and wanted for her dream home.

The streets had been good to DJ, and his team as well. Angelo took more notice of how well DJ was doing and helped him invest his money in small real estate. DJ purchased three rental properties, opened a motorcycle and bicycle repair shop where he also bought and sold used bikes, and purchased a beauty salon. Things were good.

DJ was invited to Detroit for a hair and nail show. The convention was to last the weekend, so he took Show and Habit along with him, leaving Tommy to hold things down until they returned.

CHAPTER 16

The Cheetah Club was a popular strip club that was jumping from wall to wall with lap dances, pole dancers, and guys trying to get the girls to leave with them. Three men sat in their favorite corner enjoying the show onstage by a sexy creamy stripper. They liked the table because it gave them a prefect view of both the stage and the entrance.

"Would you like a dance?" the sexy, tall, thick dancer asked.

"Hell yeah, ma! Show a nigga what you workin' with!" Spank answered, right away peeling off a few bills from the wad of cash he was holding.

The scantily dressed girl spun right around giving him a good view of her big butt, before making it dance and clap for him. She twirled back around and hopped onto Spank's lap. He cupped her breasts, and she wrapped her caramel arms around his head, burying his face between them. Spank was so caught up that he didn't see Boss walk up.

"Nigga, I see you got your hands full with all that right there!" Boss said, announcing himself as he took a seat at the table.

He dapped the other two men at the table who were also enjoying the show the dancer was putting on.

"What's good, Boss! You find out something good 'bout that nigga, DJ?" Hood asked, in between trying to cop free feels of the girl's butt.

"Whoa, nigga, not now! Wait 'til this bitch gets somewhere," he responded before he pulled out a freshly rolled blunt and lit it.

"Right, right, right! Let me hit that there, folk. It smells like that dro."

"And you know it is!" Boss said with his lungs filled with the smoke.

It seemed like the weed smoke was the all call for the dancers, because once they put it in the air, three more girls rushed the table. Boss wasn't going to let the attention go to waste. He and the others got the tips flowing for the girls. One of the girls who was there just to try to buy a blunt from them quickly parked her fat ass in Boss's lap. He not only sold her a bag of weed, but he also set up a date with her for later. After two more songs passed, the girls moved on to the next big spenders, giving the guys the time they needed to talk.

"Folks, I know where the nigga lay his head at night."

"Straight up! How you get that info?" Spank asked Boss before he took a sip of his beer while eyeing a new girl onstage.

"I followed his bitch from the daycare the other day. I saw her when I was over on 28th fucking with Ed. How I knew it was her is because she was driving the nigga's truck. So I followed the hoe."

"Y'all know that nigga just opened that beauty shop on Fond du Lac, so I bet he's going to that big hair show in the D tomorrow," Hood told them. "Hell, I'm trying to go, and I ain't got a damn shop."

"Say, folk, we doing this to get money, so don't be on that bullshit you was on way back when!" Boss warned Spank, who was still playing peek-a-boo with the girl onstage.

"Yeah, ole stupid-ass nigga! You lucky ol' girl didn't see your face. Your fool ass gonna catch something you don't want doing that thirsty shit!" D-town told him.

"Hey, nigga, don't hate! It's what I do, and the bitches love me," Spank responded with a proud smile on his face.

"Yeah, they love you in your head, ole fool-ass nigga!" Rio snapped.

Boss then laid out the plan he had in mind for the robbery.

* * *

The heavy door slammed behind Meka when she rushed out of the house to her car. She had to pick up her best friend from the airport and didn't want to be late or miss her expression when she stepped off the plane. The smell of grass and fertilizer was strong in the air from the light rain storm the night before. Meka jogged across the lawn to the 1998 Honda Accord parked in front of the garage. The car belonged to her sister-in-law. For some reason, her Lexus RX330 wouldn't start for her this morning.

When Meka reached the car, a man in a mask materialized behind her, and another sprang up from hiding between the cars and pointed a gun in her face. The sight of the two men alone caused her heart to skip and her to freeze with fear.

"Bitch, don't say a muthafuckin word!" one of the men warned as he took hold of her arm and pushed his gun hard in her back.

"Good, now let's go back into the house," the other said as they walked Meka forcefully back inside.

Once inside, the man holding her demanded to know who else was in the house.

"Nobody! Just me. Ain't nobody else here," she lied, trying to protect Lisa, who was somewhere upstairs. "There ain't shit here. I got like a *G* in my purse. Take it and just go. I won't call the police."

At the mention of the police, Meka was hit in the head with the gun that was being pressed against her back. The blow dazed her and caused her eyes to tear. The guy holding her then forced her upstairs to the bedrooms. Meka couldn't see what part of the house the other guy went into. She prayed he stayed downstairs to give her a better chance. He did just that, and with the odds a little better, Meka planed her next move.

She still had her purse over her shoulder. Inside it was her .25 automatic. Her mind was racing as she tried to look for the right place to make her move. Before she could finish her thought, she was hit in the back of the head again. This time the blow felt like she was hit with a hammer, which caused her to stumble and drop her purse onto the floor.

"Bitch, if you wanna live, you'll tell me what I wanna know— and

that is where the fuckin' money and shit's at. Show me the fuckin' safe!"

"I don't know. I don't live here. This ain't my house. I told you that there ain't shit in here!" she explained to him as her terror mounted.

This time she was punched in her lower back, and she responded with an elbow to his rib cage. And the fight was on. Meka thrust herself forward trying her best to flip the gunman off of her, but he was too heavy for her. He put her in a chokehold, which began cutting off her air. Meka continued to fight, only making him increase the pressure of the hold and restricting the blood flow to her head. Meka felt herself getting lightheaded. She stomped down as hard as she could on his foot, causing him to release her long enough to punch her in her back again. Meka knew she couldn't fight too much longer. She was going to die if she didn't do something fast. The fear of death mixed with anger gave her the strength to force herself up, and she hit him hard on the chin with her head. The blow dazed him, and he loosened his hold. As soon as Meka felt the blood returning to her head, she tried to flip him off of her again but with no luck. So she threw her elbow back in his face repeatedly until she heard a crunching sound.

"Awwww! Bitch, you broke my fuckin' nose!" he cried and

cursed, retightening his hold and shaking her by her neck with the force of a bear.

He dropped her when he heard her neck snap. Meka felt her body sag and go cold before she passed out from the pain.

He tossed her body to the floor and then went in search of what he had come for. He trashed the room, flipping over the bed, pulling out the dressers, and tossing everything around inside the closet. He was going through the shoe boxes when he heard a female's voice coming from somewhere outside of the room, followed by a gunshot. The shot made him drop what he was doing and flee the house.

CHAPTER 17

Princess browsed through the crowded airport in search of Meka's smiling face. After almost an hour had passed with no Meka or having anyone return her calls, Princess went outside and flagged down a cab.

"I know this damn girl didn't forget about me," she said to herself before she gave the driver the address she was given just in case something like this happened. "I guess being away four years is long enough to be forgotten."

She shook her head and dropped back in the seat of the cab as it pulled away. The driver took the longest way he could to get to his destination. Princess wasn't upset when he finally pulled to a stop in front of the address. She enjoyed the small tour of her hometown and was amazed by all of the changes. She paid the driver after denying his offer to carry her bags to the door for her for the second time, along with his request for her phone number. She then stepped out into the sun that seemed to be on blast all of a sudden. It did feel weird to her to be walking up to DJ and his wife's home—a home that Princess wished she had with him.

Princess had a nice talk with Lisa over the phone and found out she was pretty cool. Lisa told Princess how much the twins talked about her all the time. She even admitted that DJ was hurt when she just up and left him. Princess wanted to believe she was still a part of their lives no matter what had happened between her and DJ, and stressed just that to Lisa, who gave her the okay to come to their home. But somewhere deep down, Lisa just wanted to be sure DJ was over his ex, and to see if Princess was still as pretty as she was in the photos Meka had of the three of them, hanging on the wall at her place.

The door was slightly ajar, giving Princess the idea that the twins had set her up for a surprise. So she eased the door open and peeked inside to announce that she had made it. But when she pushed the door open, she found a woman lying face down in a pool of blood. She dropped her bags and ran to see if the woman was still alive. She wasn't. Princess couldn't believe that this wasn't a bad dream.

She then heard a noise coming from upstairs and quickly drew her gun from her purse and went to go investigate. Princess started carrying a gun ever since the night of the rape. She took two types of self-defense classes in Atlanta along with going to the shooting range every weekend to make sure she knew how to properly use a gun. She found Meka on the floor halfway in a bedroom doorway struggling to breathe.

"Oh my God, Meka! Who did this to you!" she screamed, rushing to her side as she pulled out her cell phone to call for help.

She felt how cold Meka's body was, so she snatched a blanket off the floor of the ransacked bedroom and covered her with it. Princess sat on the floor with her back to the wall with her best friend until she heard the police announce they were inside the house.

"I'm up here! Please hurry! I need help! She's still alive!" she yelled with her voice full of fear.

"Please put down the gun, ma'am, and let us get her some help."

"Okay, don't shoot," Princess said as she placed her gun on the floor. "I'm the one who called."

"Is there anyone else here?" the officer asked as he picked up the gun and allowed the EMTs inside to help Meka.

"No!" she answered, feeling sick to her stomach as she walked passed Lisa's dead body.

Although she didn't know her like that, it hurt as if she did.

"Just a little longer and this one wouldn't need a doctor," one of the EMTs said as they carried Meka out to the ambulance.

Princess was about to jump inside and ride in the ambulance with Meka, but she spotted a daycare van pulling up to drop off Lisa's daughters at home. She then explained to the van driver, Terrisa, what had happened.

"Oh my goodness! You go ahead to the hospital, I got them. I run a daycare at my home, so I'll keep them until you can pick them up," Terrisa told her, leaving Princess with her phone numbers.

Since the ambulance had already left, Princess jumped inside Lisa's car after seeing the keys in the door. As she sped to the county hospital, she thought of the confused faces of the two little girls who just lost their mother and didn't know it. By the time she made it to her destination, Princess had made her mind up that she would do whatever was necessary for the kids and stay as long as DJ needed her to.

She rushed inside the hospital's emergency room entrance and was happy that it was not very crowded. This gave Princess more hope that her friend was immediately getting the help she needed. She talked to a nurse, who pointed her toward the waiting room. After about ten minutes, two detectives approached Princess and wanted to ask her more questions about the incident. She remembered one of them from the house, but the other was new to her.

"It's a good thing you got there when you did. You know we have to hold on to your gun until it's cleared, and I gotta ask that you don't leave the city before then."

"Okay. How long will it be before I get my gun back?"

"You'll have it as soon as the techs are done with it. Why the rush?" the detective she didn't recognize asked while looking at her with suspicion in his pale blue eyes.

Princess knew he was trying to pick with her, but she didn't give in.

"Okay, whatever! I'm not going nowhere."

She sat down and dropped her head, hoping they would understand the conversation was over.

"Oh, one more thing before we go. Did you take a car from the house? One of the witnesses told us they saw the deceased's car speeding away shortly after a daycare van pulled away."

"Yeah, that was me. I saw the keys and just took it. I didn't know who the car belonged to. I'm sorry. If you need to take it, take it."

"No, I think we're good. I was just following up on it."

He put away his note pad.

"Please have the husband give us a call as soon as you can, so we can clear him."

With that said, they walked out of the waiting room, leaving Princess alone with her thoughts. She looked up and saw the nurse she had spoken with earlier when she arrived.

"Hey, excuse me. Do you remember me from earlier?"

"Yes. Do you need something?" the nurse asked, stopping to talk with her.

"I just wanna know what's going on with my friend, Dameka Johns?"

"I'll check in with the doctor, but to be honest right now, it still would be too early to know much. But let me check and get back to you, okay?"

Princess went back into the waiting room and got down on her knees to pray that Meka would be okay. She begged the Lord to give her the strength to do everything necessary for her friends. The nurse returned an hour later and told her it was still too early to know anything and that she should go home and get some rest.

But rest was the last thing on Princess's mind when she returned to the house. She needed to get in touch with DJ, but didn't have a number to reach him. She looked around the house for Lisa's cell phone, hoping the police hadn't taken it like they did Meka's. She didn't find it, but she did find a number for DJ's hotel room on a note pad next to the kitchen phone. She called and left a message for him to call her back at his house or to come home right away. She wondered how she was going to tell him his wife was dead and his sister was in the hospital fighting for her life.

Princess busied herself by cleaning up the blood and mess the police made. She didn't want to bring the twins to the house the way it was. They were much too young to understand death and what was going on, or even that their mother was never coming home. When she was satisfied with her cleaning job, she called Terrisa and asked if she could stop by and pick up the girls. Terrisa told Princess she would drop them off to her since she was already out with them.

When the kind woman arrived at DJ's house with the children, Princess offered to pay her. Terrisa turned down the money, but she told her she would be happy to take care of the girls if she or the family needed her.

"Do you mind praying with me, Princess?"

"Yeah, Lord knows we need it right now."

They held hands as Terrisa prayed.

"Oh Lord, almighty Father God. Protect us and enlighten our lives. Lord, please be with my sisters, Princess and Dameka. Father, please bring her home alive and well. Give sista Princess the strength she needs to do what needs to be done for those two babies. Oh Lord, we come to you with our hearts open, so hear our prayer. Forever and ever, Amen!"

The two shared a much-needed hug after the prayer. Terrisa then got in her van and vanished into the night, leaving Princess with the twins, who were still sleeping from when they were brought into the house. Princess stood over them admiring how much they looked like their father. Princess never thought she would return to something as tragic as this, but she also never thought she would return to the city of Milwaukee at all.

Around 3:00 a.m., she was awakened by the ringing of the phone next to the couch on which she had fallen asleep.

"Hello?"

"Who is this?"

"Domeko, it's me, Princess."

"Hey, you! Why you answering my house phone at this time of night, and when did you make it back?"

"DJ? DJ!" she raised her voice to hush his questioning. "Did you get my message telling you to come home?"

"No, all I got was the number to call home. Why, what's wrong?"

"You need to get here right now. Dameka's in the hospital and Lisa is—is—!"

Princess's voice faded as she tried to bring herself to tell him about his wife.

"Hello? Hello?"

"I'm here."

"Where's Lisa, Princess?" he demanded, with his voice full of worry.

"I'm so sorry, Meko. She's dead. I found her when I got here."

Princess told him and tears began pouring from her eyes.

"What! She's what, Princess?" he shouted into the phone, getting his guys' attention.

"She's dead. Someone shot her. The police think it was a robbery gone wrong," she explained the best she could.

"Hello, Princess? This is Show. What's going on over there?" he asked when he picked the phone up off the floor where DJ had dropped it.

"Show, it's all bad. Y'all need to get here now, and I'll explain the whole story then. Tell Meko I got the twins and they're fine, but get here as fast as y'all can."

"Okay, baby girl. We on our way, and I'm sending Tommy over there until we make it," he told her before hanging up the phone.

Princess started crying harder after the call with DJ, because once again she had broken his heart.

CHAPTER 18

DJ passed along to his guys what he had been told by Princess before his heart broke and he dropped the phone. After pacing the room trying to clear his head, DJ called Angelo and explained what had happened.

"Man, I need to get there quick. Like now! Can you send your plane to get us?"

"My plane will take too long to get there from here, but I got you. I'll have one waiting for you ready to go at the airport," Angelo promised before he called to charter a private flight for them without a second thought about it.

On the plane, Habit called Tommy to have someone at the airport pick them up when they landed. Habit was the only one of the three of them who could think straight. DJ was sitting in a daze. His face was tight with anger and shock. Show wasn't far behind him. He was also sick with worry over what had happened. Show and Meka had made their relationship official the year after Princess moved away, and they had been together for the past two years. He wanted blood and wouldn't stop until he got it.

When they got off the plane, Zoe was there waiting for them. Habit ordered him to get the bags, and then the three took his car and left Zoe at the airport.

DJ stormed through the city racing to get home, almost getting into a collision with a city bus. When they walked into the house, they almost didn't recognize Princess. She wasn't the skinny girl that she was before she left. Princess was now country thick and wore her hair in long micro-braids. They found her in the family room sitting on the floor playing with the twins.

"Daddy, Daddy!" they yelled as soon as they noticed DJ standing there.

The girls dropped what they were doing and ran into his arms. He held them as they tried to tell him about their new friend, Princess.

"Hey, Princess, let's go over here and talk," Show said, leading her away from DJ and the kids.

"Okay," she agreed without taking her eyes off of DJ and his kids.

She could see the pain in his face as he fought back tears while listening to his babies. Princess explained to Show and Habit from the beginning all the events that she knew. DJ had sent Tommy back to pick up Zoe from the airport and had Princess tell him the story again. She snapped out of her thoughts of their unborn child. Seeing DJ with the twins triggered feelings she wasn't sure she wanted to be feeling.

"The police said there had to be at least two of them to do it because of the tracks they found on the kitchen floor, and that it was most likely someone they knew."

DJ looked at the men in the room with him, but he shook off the thought that one of his own could have done this to him.

"Where's my sister?"

Princess told him what hospital Meka had been admitted to.

"Meko, you go. I'll stay here and take care of the girls as long as you need me to. It's time for them to get ready for daycare anyway," she told him.

Princess and Terrisa thought it would be best for the kids to continue with their set routines. She explained their suggestion to DJ before taking the girls up to their room to get ready to go when the van arrived to pick them up.

DJ and the others sat in the family room trying to take in

everything Princess had told them. No one could believe this had happened.

"I'm going to the hospital," Show stated after jumping to his feet.

"Yeah, I'm going with you. Hab, would you stay here with—?"

"Bro, you know I got you. Call me and let me know how sis is doing," Habit said while walking out to the garage with them.

* * *

"I'ma kill them muthafuckas' families who did this shit!" Show snapped as he drove them to the county hospital.

"I don't understand why they shot them. Why'd they kill Lisa? She would've given them whatever they wanted. There's about fifty *G*s in the house I keep just in case of emergencies."

"Did Princess say they took the money or anything?"

"I don't think she did, and I didn't look around the house like that."

"Call her and tell her to check."

"I'm doing that right now," DJ said, pulling out his cell phone.

When she answered, he told her what to do and where to look for the money.

"It's still here. It don't even look like it's been touched."

"Okay. You can use that if you need something, Princess, and thank you for staying."

He told Show that it was still there, and they continued to rack their brains until they pulled into the hospital.

Once inside, they were taken to meet with the doctor assigned to Meka. The doctor told them he had to finish up with another call, and he would then talk with them right afterward. In the meantime, DJ had to fill out paperwork for his sister's care. While he was dealing with the nurse, Show was on the phone with their guys. He put the word out that they wanted the ones who did this, and he announced a reward of $5,000 to anyone who had real information for them. DJ told Show to add that he had a $100,000 for the ones who killed his wife, dead or alive.

"What did the doc say 'bout Meka?" Show asked as they walked up the stairs, because the elevator was taking too long to get to them.

"He said she don't got control of her body right now, but he still has some tests to run before knows for sure if she's gonna be paralyzed."

DJ had to blink back tears as he explained.

"She ain't even breathing on her own?"

Show was speechless thinking of his lover and friend not being able to do for herself again. It was hard to believe, and he hated himself for not answering the phone for her while he was getting sucked off by one of the hair-show models at the after-party.

Meka's room was cool and dimly lit. The only sound was the beeping of the many machines to which she was connected. When DJ and Show walked inside, the smell of disinfectants and medicine filled their noses. Show couldn't believe this was his woman lying in front of him, and DJ's heart hesitated when he saw his sister with a thick clear tube through the base of her throat.

As they stepped closer, they could see she was being held down by a white plastic body brace connected to the bed and that she had two IVs, one in each arm. Her face was badly swollen, and her eyes were so puffy that they looked like razor slits. Meka's skin was even an ugly nameless color. Seeing her like this only added to the anger they were already feeling. Neither of them wanted to be in the room. But before they turned to leave, Meka opened her eyes as much as she could and saw them standing there before they closed again.

She couldn't talk because of the tube in her throat, but she could hear them talking to her as she faded in and out of consciousness.

"Dameka?" DJ started as he struggled to control his emotions. "I'm here. I don't know if you can hear me or not, but I love you. Just don't give up on me. I promise I'ma kill them niggas that did this to you. I promise to God I am!"

With that said, Meka opened her eyes again breaking her brother's heart even more. DJ could not take it any longer and walked out of the room, leaving Show alone with her to say what he needed.

"Hold on, baby! I can't lose you. I love you and know you're stronger than this. Meka, you told me that you's a bad bitch, remember? Well, I need you to show me you are and come out from under this shit here!"

A single tear slipped from his eye and onto Meka's face. He noticed it when he kissed her forehead.

* * *

The return trip to DJ's home was done in silence as both of the hate-filled men recalled happier times they shared with Meka and Lisa. DJ thought of how his sister always had his back when they were kids, and the many times she had blackmailed him into getting what she wanted in return for not telling their mom whatever he had gotten into at the time. He remembered how beautiful Lisa looked when he made her his wife and when she gave birth to the twins.

He thought of how they met and the way she made him feel when they made love. DJ couldn't believe his wife was gone and his sister may never walk again or have children of her own. He took a second to glance at Show. He could see the pain in his face as clear as his own.

Show dipped and swung the truck through the streets thinking of all of the times he shared with Meka and Lisa. His hate mounted the more he thought of all of the women he had cheated on her with whenever they had a fight. He didn't cheat because he didn't love her, but because he needed to feel like he still had control of his heart. The truth was his heart only belonged to Meka. She had him from the first time he laid eyes on her on Wells. She and Princess were riding in her little beat-up Ford and pulled up on him and DJ to get money for gas or something like that. Show wanted to get her attention, so he gave her $20 and told her to make sure to put something good in her smart mouth. He thought of the way Lisa would make a fuss about him always coming over and drinking the twins' Juicy Juice.

Before they turned back down DJ's block, both of their minds were on murder. At the house, Tommy and Zoe refused to leave DJ home alone, so DJ gave in to them and allowed Zoe to stay the night. Tommy and Show took off back to the ghetto to begin the hunt for answers.

Princess gave the kids their baths, and DJ put them to bed. He was sitting in the dark of their room when he got a call from Angelo telling him he had sent his people to find who had done this to his friends. He also told DJ he had put another $100,000 with the reward that was already out on the streets.

"DJ, use the cash from our last run to make all of this happen. I'm very sorry for your loss, and like I told you in the beginning, I take care of my family." Angelo went on to say that he was sick of the game and things happening to his family. "When this is over, I think I'm done, but we will speak of that later. Right now, let's stay on task."

"DJ, come and let me fix you something to eat," Princess yelled through the closed bedroom door, where DJ had taken the call so he wouldn't wake the girls.

"Okay, give me a second! I'm on the phone!"

After he ended the call, he joined her and Zoe in the dinner room. Princess had made Southern fried chicken, red beans and rice, and her grandmother's cornbread. DJ wasn't really hungry, but he ate what he could as they talked about old times and the kids. Everything but what had happened the day before.

"Hey, y'all, I'ma be outside in the car smoking if ya need me," Zoe said, excusing himself from the conversation to go do his job of making sure the would-be robbers, or whoever did this, didn't return.

DJ continued talking with Princess, and soon his thoughts were of how much he missed her. He also couldn't help admiring how good she looked, even though he felt ashamed for his thoughts. How could he be thinking of her the way he was, when he had just lost his wife. But he couldn't deny the connection between them was still there.

CHAPTER 19

The King family blamed DJ for their daughter's death and didn't allow him to attend the funeral. DJ didn't try to fight with them, since he felt they had every right to be mad at him. He still paid for everything and made sure his wife still had the best in death as she did in life. Princess stepped up and took the twins to see their mother off, with DJ watching and saying his goodbyes from a safe distance across the cemetery.

During the days leading up to and long after the funeral, DJ's drinking steadily increased. He spent almost all of his time in the streets looking for any little bit of information about the home invasion. DJ stopped spending time with his kids, and he stopped going to visit Meka at the hospital.

* * *

After about two months, everything just came down on him, and he gave up on it all. DJ would no longer come out of his bedroom.

Princess stuck with her promise and took care of the house and the kids like they were her own. The twins had fallen right in rhythm with her, which made her job easy. Princess had thought of going to

Meka's house to stay, but she didn't want to be too far away from DJ and the kids. With the way DJ was acting these days, there was no way she could leave and believe the girls would be safe. It was hard for her to be in the house with DJ knowing she was still very much in love with him. At times, she thought he still loved her too. She tried her best to comfort him. In fact, Princess did everything she could to get through to DJ.

Terrisa became a good friend and would keep the girls while Princess went to the hospital to visit Meka and when she went to make the trips to the state line to meet Carlo in DJ's place.

Princess held things down the best she could with the help of Tommy and Show. Show had gotten Princess permission to have Meka moved to a private room in the hospital since DJ wasn't talking to them unless they had information for him. Princess okayed the move. She told Show to do what he felt was best.

One night she was reading to Meka at the side of her bed when Meka moved her fingers on her left hand. Princess wasn't sure she had witnessed it, and waited, almost holding her breath until it happened again. As soon as it did, she hurried out of the room and got the nearest doctor she found and almost dragged him back into the room. When they returned, Meka was opening and closing her hand over and over. Princess immediately tried calling DJ on his cell phone, but he didn't answer. She then tried the landline, but he still wouldn't answer, so she called Show.

"What up? Who is this?"

"Show, Meka's moving her hands!" Princess almost screamed into the phone excitedly.

"What? I'm on my way!" he told her, not attempting to hide the excitement in his voice.

"Hold up, Show. I need you to go see about Domeko, because I can't get him on the phone."

"P, I got him right here with me. He's in the truck. We'll be there in a few," Show promised before ending the call.

"Bro, where we gonna be in a minute?" DJ asked, overhearing Show's conversation.

"That was Princess. She's at the hospital and said Meka's moving her hands," he explained as he climbed behind the wheel of his truck and sped off toward the hospital.

* * *

At the hospital, Princess was waiting for them in the lobby.

She led them to the family waiting area and then explained that the doctors had kicked her out of the room so they could do their jobs. Show had gotten a page and walked outside to have a smoke and return the call.

"Why didn't you answer my call, Domeko?" Princess asked once they were alone.

"I was busy," he answered coldly.

"Did I do something wrong or something, because for the past few days you haven't said two words to me, and I've been doing everything. You wouldn't come out for me or your kids, but you're out with Show! How in the fuck do you think that makes me feel?"

DJ took a step away from her.

"Look, let's not do this right now. I promise we'll talk at home, okay?"

Princess was so upset that she just walked off toward the restrooms, just as Show rushed back in.

"Bro, Habit just said he got some females over on 61st and Carmen who claim to know something about what had happened. I already sent Tommy and Zoe out there to check it out."

"Let's run over there."

"No, you stay here and find out what's going on. I'ma go because this waiting shit is killing me!" Show told DJ.

DJ thought about the talk he just had with Princess.

"I got you on that. I hope them hoes ain't on no bullshit just trying to get some money and shit."

"I'ma find out," Show said before he walked out the door, almost running into Princess.

"What's up? Where you going?"

"I may have some news on that shit. I'll be right back," he told her and moved on out the door.

CHAPTER 20

About an hour or so after Show rushed off out the waiting room door, two people dressed in white hospital gear walked in. It was the doctor and a nurse. The doctor looked tired and was carrying large X-ray photos in one hand and a hot cup of coffee in the other. The nurse / was also holding coffee, only she had brought it for the three of them.

"What is it?" DJ demanded before the doctor could get all the way in the room.

"Is she gonna be alright?" Princess asked before the doctor could answer the first question.

"Excuse me, but weren't there three of you? I thought you might need a pick-me-up?" the nurse said, offering them the coffees.

The doctor thanked her with his eyes for giving him time to gather his thoughts.

"Oh yeah, he had to go," Princess told her, not missing the look of disappointment.

It made her wonder if Show knew the nurse or if she was just hoping to get to him.

"There are still some more tests to run, but if you follow me next door, I would like to show you her X-rays," the doctor told them, holding up the sheets in his hand before turning and walking out the door with the others following.

In the other room the doctor put up the X-ray photos and pointed to the first one.

"See this right here?" he touched the area that he wanted them to see with his finger. "At first sight, I thought it was shattered bone, but now look at this one that was just taken today."

"It's gone. I don't see it anymore," Princess mumbled.

"So what does it mean? Is my sister going to be alright?"

The doctor smiled at DJ and said, "It looks very hopeful. I would like to send her to a specialist down in Texas. I think his work will help speed up your sister's healing and have her back on her feet in no time."

DJ told the doctor to do whatever he had to for Meka, before giving him a grateful handshake.

"Can we see her now?" Princess asked.

"I think you should let her rest for now. I gave her something to relax her so she wouldn't hurt herself. She's breathing on her own, and we don't want to excite her. She's a real fighter," the doctor answered, just as they heard his name being paged over the hospital's loudspeaker.

The doctor and nurse excused themselves and rushed off to wherever they were called.

"She's gonna be okay!" DJ said excitedly, pulling Princess into his arms and kissing her on the lips a bit longer than he intended. "I'ma go call Show and tell him."

DJ then quickly walked out of the room.

The simple kiss had aroused Princess. Her panties were moist. She wanted him so much that the slight touch was too much for her. Princess wondered if there was any hope for them getting back together.

* * *

Show made it across the city in no time. He didn't have to look hard for the house on Carmen Street, because both Habit's van and Tommy's car were parked right out front with Zoe and another one of their guys posted outside. Zoe flagged down Show to make sure he saw them.

"Tommy and Hab are in the house. I think these hoes might

know something for real, big bro," Zoe reported as he escorted Show inside.

The inside of the two women's home was cozy. Things were neat and in place as if someone older owned the place rather than the two women sitting in front of Show. He asked them to tell him what they had already told the others from the beginning. The women didn't complain, knowing there was a big reward for the information they had.

"We dance at the Cheetah Club whenever we're in town," the slim, average-height, wavy redhead explained with her cell phone clutched tightly in her hand.

"Well, these two niggas named Rio and D-town were there last night flashing their cash and trying to get a date for the night. Since the club was slow and about to close in an hour, I let her talk me into it," she said, referring to her roommate, a shorter, honey-blonde, thick-legged girl sitting to the right of her.

She was nursing a glass of gin in one hand and a blunt between her fill lips.

"We brought them here because they were drunk and giving up that cash. While she was putting on a striptease for them, they started talking to each other saying they wish they could've gotten that nigga DJ. I came out of the kitchen when I heard that 'cuz I heard one of the other girls saying something about DJ and y'all having a reward out for info on who tried to rob him or something."

"It's more than that, but did they say anything about a shooting or anything else?" Show questioned.

"No, not really. I tried to get them to talk about it more, but they was too busy trying to fuck."

"What you mean not really?"

"The one that was running off at the mouth kept calling the other a dumb trigger-happy nigga. But they were talking about two things at the same time. Well, that's how it sounded to me," the short girl stated.

The strippers went on with the story, adding that they were supposed to meet up with them at the club again that night around twelve thirty. Show didn't know how to take the info, but it was the best he had heard since the mess had happened. He noticed that the girls didn't say much about the reward money, and he realized they didn't know how much it was. He gave them $500 each with the promise that they would get the rest if what they said checked out.

"Here's another $500 if y'all call us as soon as them niggas walk into the club," he told them, trying to make it look a bit sweeter to the gold-diggers.

"Yeah, we got you!" the redhead agreed, accepting the bonus cash.

"Is you gonna stay and kick it, or do you gotta go now?" she asked Habit.

He looked at Show to see what he should do. Show shrugged his shoulders and smiled.

"You know I'm trying to kick it. Is your girl trying to get down, 'cuz my nigga outside is trying to kick it too."

Show sent in Bam and Zoe when he got outside. He called DJ from inside his truck after noticing he had a few missed calls from him. The two men swapped information as he drove home. Show relayed what the girls had told him about Rio and D-town, and his plan to catch them at the club. DJ told him about the doctor wanting to send Meka to Texas for treatment. He then asked Show to pick him up from the house because he had ridden back with Princess.

* * *

DJ barely noticed the pounding bass as he went over all of what

177

Show had told him when he picked him up from the house. They were now sitting in the strip club waiting for Rio and his guys to show up. Just before DJ and Show went inside, DJ called Tommy.

"What up, bro?"

"Get Zoe and come down to the Cheetah Club. I want y'all to find a spot outside and lay low. I need to know as soon as them hoe-ass niggas pull up."

"Lil' bro's right here, so we on our way. All is well!"

"Mighty!" DJ responded before he ended the call.

"You ready, bro?" Show asked him before they got out of the truck.

DJ removed his gun and laid it on the floor of the truck.

"Yeah, let's go," he answered before he got out.

Show laid one of his guns on the floor close to the door of the truck so he could get to it easily if he needed it. He then followed him into the club. The place had typical bad lighting, and a bouncer sat on a stool just inside the entrance. Another man sat behind a table with a cash register and a hand stamp on it. Both men wore black T-shirts, gray army fatigue pants, and black boots. DJ paid for the both of them and let the bouncer pat him and Show down. They then walked over to the far end of the bar and waved the bartender over to them.

The Cheetah Club's walls were filled with neon beer signs and posters of topless women posing on classic muscle cars and motorcycles. The rest of the walls were covered with mirrors to let the patrons see the stage from almost anywhere they sat. Show ordered two double shots of Patrón and two beers for the both of them, while DJ looked around the club for anyone he knew. The bartender pulled down the bottle of tequila from the neatly filled shelf and filled their order. He then moved on to the other end of the bar where he was talking to one of the sexy dancers that was on a break or waiting for her turn to go onstage. DJ watched one of the stripper's hips as she walked over to them.

"Hey, Show! Y'all early. I didn't expect to see you so soon," Honey said.

"We wanted to be here as soon as they got here, so we won't miss them. Is they here yet?"

"No, not yet. But here, I pulled this off my cell. I forgot I took it last night," she said as she handed him a photo of the guys they were looking for on the low.

DJ pulled out a wad of cash from his pocket and tipped her $300.

"Thank you. This don't got shit to do with the reward either."

Honey happily accepted the money.

"If there's something else I can do, just let me know," she told them before she blew them kisses and put an extra twist in her hips for them as she walked away.

Show noticed when the other girl they met on Carmen Street took the stage and began her set. But he wasn't really watching her show or the other girls working the floor of the club. He was looking for the men who hurt his queen.

An hour had passed without seeing either of the men, and Show's anger got the best of him as did the drinks.

He grabbed a bouncer who he thought was challenging him and slammed him against the bar. In one motion, DJ pulled a second gun that Show didn't know he was carrying and pressed it under the big man's chin. The bartender didn't notice the action at the other end of the bar, because he was too caught up in what the girl was telling him. The strippers that were sitting not far from them quickly moved out of the way, but they continued to shuffle through the men in the club simply minding their own business.

"Okay, man, you got me! Don't kill me!" the bouncer pleaded.

"Have you seen this nigga in here tonight?" Show asked, shoving the photo in his face.

"Yeah, man, I've seen him before, but not tonight."

"Do you know where he'd be at? Where can I find him or a muthafucka he knows?" DJ asked, easing up on his hold a bit.

"Man, I don't know shit about him. I just work here, but I think that hoe at the pool table fucks with him."

They released the man after seeing that the female at the pool table was Honey.

"Hey, homie, we good. I just need to get up with these niggas. It ain't got shit to do with you," DJ explained to the shaken bouncer before handing him a $100 bill.

"DJ! DJ!"

DJ turned toward the familiar voice coming from over by the entrance.

"Rain? What good? What you doing in here?" he asked as his friend from HOC approached them.

"You know me. I fucks with the bitches, my nigga. I'm at where the bitches at. I got a hoe or two in here," Rain answered, shaking

DJ's hand. "I ain't seen you down this way before. And like I said, I'm in this spot all the time."

"I'm looking for these niggas," DJ said as he took the photo from Show and showed it to Rain.

"Ah shit, my nigga, that fool-ass nigga and his guys are always in here. They should be falling through in a minute. Hold up! Gimme a sec to check in with my bitches, and I'll be right back at you."

"No rush!" DJ responded, looking at the bouncer they roughed up to make sure he wasn't on nothing sneaky.

They looked on as Rain collected cash from two of the dancers working the club. He must've told them DJ and Show were off limits to whatever hustle they were putting down, because the girls stopped eyeing them.

"Hey, let a nigga know if y'all looking for something sexy for an after-party or anything," he told them when he returned.

"Let's go outside, I need to run some shit past you, and I might need your help," DJ told him.

"Alright, it's whatever with me."

Once they stepped outside, DJ introduced Show to Rain, telling Show how they met. He then explained to Rain what went down that had them looking for the guys in the photo.

"This is the best lead we done had so far."

"I heard about that shit, but you never crossed my mind. I can't believe them stupid-ass muthafuckas tried to rob you and killed your people," Rain said as he shook his head. "Fuck them bitches! Like I said, I heard about all of this, but you, my nigga. So fuck that lil' cash you got out there on them. Just let me know what you need me to do," he told them before removing his Glock to show them he was armed.

"Well, if they show up tonight, they've fucked up again!" DJ told him.

"Yeah, we got somebody trying to find out where they lay their heads right now just in case they don't," Show added.

A car tapped its horn as it stopped next to them. It was Tommy and Zoe followed by Habit in his 1974 bloodied Fleetwood sitting on 24-inch flats.

"What you doing here?" DJ asked as all seven men stood outside of the club parked at the edge of the lot.

"I know you niggas didn't think I was just gonna sit this shit out. Fuck that! DJ, you handled that shit for me when them niggas shot off my leg, and Meka always kept a bad bitch around to help take care of a nigga. That punk shit hurt me, too," Habit explained while shifting his weight onto his good leg.

"Y'all know I been hitting these bricks from day one on this shit. Now I need to kill me a muthafucka!" Trouble said.

"Like you always say, we family, so we all we got. When one hurts, we all feel it, so together we gonna deal with it," Tommy butted in from his position sitting on the hood of the car.

It filled DJ and Show with pride to have these men with them ready to kill or be killed for their loved ones. But DJ's mind was still made up. He was out of the game when all of this was over. He made plans to make sure everyone would be taken care of before he went, but he was done.

CHAPTER 21

Trouble received a phone call on his cell.

"Nigga, I just got an address to that nigga Rio's crib."

"Is the nigga there right now?" Show asked, standing to his full height.

"I don't know. I'ma call her and find out."

"No, fuck that! Let's just go over there and make whoever we find tell us where's he at or call him back to the house," Rain suggested. "Calling might cause that bitch to do something more than what she should if the bitch ain't trained," he explained while looking at Trouble.

"You right. Let's go!" DJ butted in before he and Show jogged over to the truck and pulled off, trailing behind Trouble and Habit with the others right behind.

It wasn't long before they were pulling over on 46th just off Sherman Boulevard. Show had been over in the area not long ago. He knew the house they were looking at was not a family home but a drug house. Once again, all of them gathered outside of the vehicles parked not far from the spot. Show told them what he knew about the house, and DJ told them how he wanted to hit it.

A black-and-silver Buick LeSabre cruised slowly up the block. The couple inside looked at them with curiosity as they passed. The car continued passing a few houses before it slid into an open parking spot. The guys waited until the couple was inside their home before they made a move.

Habit pulled out two vests from his backseat and passed the body armor over to DJ and Show. He took a second to think before he then pulled off his and gave it to Rain.

"I'm gonna be in my car, so I won't need it. Nigga, I want my shit back the way I gave it to you," Habit told Rain jokingly.

"You got it, homie. Hell, when we get done handling this shit, me and you need to sit down and talk. I need one of these joints," Rain said, pulling the vest over his head and pulling his gun. "DJ, I'm good if y'all ready."

"One of us should go see if anybody is there first, or are we just gonna run into that bitch like bro said at first?" Zoe questioned as he chambered a round into his gun.

"Here they come up the street now!" Rain announced, pointing out a marble-blue-and-gray Ford Expedition stopping in front of the house where they were going. "Yeah, that's the truck."

Show readied his gun at his side and headed toward the dark Expedition, while DJ followed. Trouble and Tommy ran across the street crouching low so they wouldn't be seen coming from the other side. Rain sprinted off between the houses so he could come from another direction, while Habit and Zoe got the cars ready for their quick escape.

The big SUV's windows were tinted so dark that it was hard to clearly identify who was inside with its interior lights on. DJ and Show had almost made it unnoticed when suddenly the doors opened and the driver looked up and saw them approaching with their guns in hand. Rio and another man took off running, just as DJ sent shots through the windows inside the truck. Tommy and Trouble were right on their heels.

Another one of DJ's shots shattered a window, and someone inside howled before he returned fire. The bullets whistled past DJ's head, but close enough for him to hear it before he dove out of the way.

Show let off a short burst before he dove out of the way of the wild spray of lead. The gunfire stopped long enough for the driver to put the truck in gear and stomp on the accelerator. They heard the tires squeal as the SUV took off. DJ didn't hesitate a second. He jumped to his feet, rapidly squeezing the trigger of his gun. The shots were coming so fast that it sounded like a fully automatic weapon until the clip emptied. Show was calmer. He took aim at the charging Expedition and put five shots through the windshield in the outline of the driver.

The truck swung violently to the right and crashed into the parked Buick that had passed them earlier.

"Slow the fuck down, bitch!" Trouble barked while aiming his gun at Rio's sweaty face.

Rio and the unknown man had split up, but the goons stayed on him.

"Don't even think about it! Hoe-ass nigga, give me a reason!" Tommy shouted as he caught up with them with his gun aimed at Rio's chest.

Rio dropped his gun and allowed them to walk him at gunpoint into the alley. Tommy made him sit on the ground while Trouble called DJ on his cell phone. Rio had other plans for his life. He rolled off of the ground onto his feet and ran as he pulled a second gun that he had hidden on his belt. He sent shots blindly behind him, hitting Trouble and causing him to lose his footing and fall hard to the ground.

Habit cut Rio off at the end of the alley with his car, but Rio didn't stop or slow. He picked up speed and hoped on top of the car. He fired once through the windshield before he leaped off the other side. That's when Rain sent shots back at Rio out of the Caddy's rear passenger window. The shots hit Rio twice in his body as he tried to take aim at the car again.

Rain got out of the car as Tommy made it to where Rio had fallen. By the time he caught up to him, someone started shooting at him from between one of the gangways as all the men ran for cover.

"Shit, who the fuck!"

"That's that other nigga that was running with him," Tommy told Rain.

They both were huddled behind a dumpster to shield themselves from his shots. Habit had smashed off after pulling Trouble into the car.

"How we gonna get outta here? We can't just sit and wait for the punk to run outta bullets!"

"I'ma try to make it over to that garage so we can get the upper hand."

"Hell, naw, nigga! You ain't gonna make it!" Rain said, knowing Tommy was thinking of making a foolish move.

"Then what! We wait until he runs up on us?"

Before Rain could answer, they heard a new gun fight start up, and they took a chance to peek out from their safe zone to see who it was. Show was sending shots wildly at the unknown man from a safe position across the street. The gunfight didn't last long because DJ had crept up behind the gunman and shot him twice in the back. Once he was down, DJ ran up on him and put one in his head to be sure he didn't get up again.

The men had just regrouped when two squad cars suddenly swung into the alley from the opposite end. Rain quickly started putting shots into the hood of the lead car, making it slam on its breaks and go in reverse. He then ran and jumped into Show's truck as they made their getaway.

CHAPTER 22

Rio's wild shots hit Trouble just outside of the vest's armor. He kept passing out as Habit raced him to the closest hospital.

Habit knew he needed to come up with a good story to tell them so they wouldn't call the police. He came to a hard stop right in front of the emergency room's entrance and started blowing his horn to get their attention inside. Two paramedics sitting in an idling ambulance ran over to see what was going on. Once Habit told them Trouble had been shot, they quickly gathered their supplies and a gurney from the ambulance. They didn't waste any more time with questions. They just pulled Trouble out of the car and instructed Habit to talk to the emergency-room staff. Since he hadn't come up with a good lie to tell them, he simply got back in his car and raced way. He called Tommy and was told that they were at the safe house on Wells, so Habit made his way there.

"So you really just left bro there by himself?" Zoe asked, shaking his head and puffing on a blunt. "Was he still alive?"

"Nigga, I told you I didn't have a choice! The nigga was in and out, so yeah he was alive when they got him. If you so bad, take your ass to the hospital with him and watch them people lock your dumb ass the fuck up until they find out what happened."

"Lil' bro, he's right. Niggas got dead tonight, and this fool shot at the police," DJ explained while pointing his beer at Rain.

"Hey, I did what I had to for us to get outta there!" Rain defended himself.

"Dude, ain't no muthafucka saying you was wrong. If it wasn't for that, we all might be in jail right now!" Show told him. "Zoe, just call that bitch he spends all his time with and send her ass down to St. Joe's to find out what's up with him. She don't know shit, so she can't tell 'em shit."

"Here, give the bitch this and tell her to keep us out of her mouth. I know they gonna ask her about his friends and shit!" DJ told Zoe as he handed him a small wad of cash.

They sat around talking shit about what they had done while smoking and drinking. Rain fell right in place with them all. DJ looked around the room and knew Lisa was with them. He felt she could rest knowing he got the ones that took her away from him and their children. He also knew it was time for him to be there for his girls. So he pulled Show to the side, away from the others, and told him he was done with the game.

"Man, bro, you tripping right now. Just chill out and think about this shit when your head is clear."

"Ain't tripping, my nigga. I'm on some whole other shit. I got to think about the twins and Dameka. I can't be out here no more. Anyway, you got this, don't you?"

"You know I got this. A nigga's been down with you from the start, so why you questioning my gangsta?"

"I'm not, big homie. I'm giving you my spot if you want it. But if you don't, I'ma have to fuck with Habit, and you know how he is!"

"Hell yeah, I want it!"

"I thought so," DJ said as he shook his hand. "I'ma set it up with Angelo so you can go down there and meet him in person. That's the way he likes to do shit even though he already knows who you is. I told him if something ever happened to me that you was next up," DJ admitted.

"So you already had this shit planned?" Show asked while shaking his head.

He was excited to be promoted, but was already missing DJ.

"Okay, I'ma take this, but you getting 10 percent of everything, and ain't no talk about that!"

"Whatever makes you happy, my nig!"

"And you don't gotta worry about Meka. I got her. As a matter of fact, let me marry her?" Show asked, holding his hand out for DJ to shake it.

"What? I don't give a fuck if you're serious. You know there's still a chance she might be in that chair for life and you need to—!"

"I don't need to think about shit. I did all the thinking I needed to when this shit first happened to us. I just want your blessing because I know she would want me to get it from you. But regardless if you give it to me or not, I'ma make it happen. I'm trying to have what you and sis had or what you got with Princess. I know I can't get there with none of these airhead hoes out here. Sure not in this life."

DJ listened as Show spoke from the heart, but the only thing that stood out from what he was saying was what he said about Princess. DJ gave in and gave Show his blessing to marry his sister before he rejoined the others.

Show decided it was best to tell the others the news after things were all set up and ready to go. He knew it would be harder to walk away from what put food on their tables and hoes in their beds.

* * *

Princess was cooking dinner for the twins. She didn't have an appetite because she was worried about DJ after watching the nightly news report. They had put up a mug shot of Trouble saying he was dropped off outside of the hospital with two gunshot wounds by an unknown man. Princess had been calling DJ's and Show's cell phones back to back whenever she could. She didn't let the twins go to school because she didn't know if their father would be coming home ever again.

"Daddy, Daddy!" Princess heard the girls yelling from the other room while she was fixing their plates.

She quickly stopped what she was doing to see if she had heard them right.

"I'm just in time. Whatever you cooked smells good. Can I have some?" DJ asked, meeting Princess at the kitchen door with both of his beautiful daughters in his arms.

Princess couldn't do anything but giggle in relief.

"Yeah, but you gotta go wash up first. Y'all two go with him so he won't run off on us again."

"We got you, Daddy."

"Put me down so I can lock the door so you can't get out."

"Hey, y'all can't just lock me in the house!" he said as he ran after his children, playing.

Princess turned around and made two more plates, one for him and the other for herself. She still didn't have her appetite, but she wasn't going to pass up having a meal with them all together.

After eating dinner and playing games, DJ helped Princess put the girls to bed. It didn't go unnoticed how well the girls behaved with Princess or how she fit right in with his family.

"Princess, can I ask you something? I need you to be open with me for real," he asked while they were having drinks and talking about the events that took place the night before.

"You can ask me whatever you want, you know that," she said while she sipped her beer.

"What happened when you took off? What was so bad that you had to get away from me?"

She took a big drink of her beer. She knew one day they would have to have this conversation.

"I didn't want you to hate me," she whispered.

"And you thought leaving me was the answer? I'm so fucking confused. You gonna have to give me more than that," he told her as he placed his drink down and faced her.

"No, I didn't know what to do. I let somebody rape me and I lost our baby. I knew you wouldn't want—!" Princess started crying.

"What do you mean you let somebody rape you? How?"

"I didn't fight as hard as I should've, and I wasn't paying mind to what I was doing."

"That wasn't your fault!" He took her hands in his. "Do you know who it was that did it?"

"No, I didn't really get a good look at his face," she answered, dropping her head.

"No, Princess, don't do that. It wasn't your fault. I wish you would've told me. You said you lost our baby?"

"Yeah, I didn't know I was—"

DJ dropped her hands and fell back into the sofa.

"Sis told me about the rape just before you came back, but not the baby. Did she know?"

"I told her not to tell you because I didn't want to hurt you. I'm so sorry, Domeko!"

He pulled Princess into his arms and hugged her tight.

"You don't have to be. I need to thank you for being here for me. I love you! I need you to know that I never stopped loving you. What I had for Lisa was just for her, like what I feel for you is just for you. I don't got no more room in my heart for nobody else. I don't know if I can do this on my own, Princess."

She looked up into his eyes. "You don't have to. I'm right here and will be as long as you need me to be."

Princess then took a chance and kissed him.

DJ returned the kiss, matching her building passion. He scooped her up while she wrapped her legs around him, never breaking their kiss. Both of them were afraid that if they stopped, the night would end. DJ carried her into the guest bedroom and placed her on the bed.

"Princess, I—!"

"Shut up!" she cut him off and started undressing him.

They quickly helped each other shed their clothes in a frantic tangle that was full of lust. Once they were naked, DJ took a moment to take in the new Princess's naked body before climbing on top of her. As they kissed and grinded together, he ran his hand up her thigh the way he did their very first time. Princess arched her back as his fingers danced in her wetness.

DJ kissed his way down her body until his lips were where his fingers once were. He then kissed and licked her just the way he remembered she liked him to, and was quickly rewarded with her sweet cum on his tongue.

"Oh shit! Oh shit! Stop!" she moaned.

DJ feared that she wasn't enjoying him. Thoughts of what she had confessed to him about the baby and rape came to mind. But then Princess pulled him back on top of her, pushing all of his doubts out of his head. She took hold of his thickness and guided it where she needed him to be.

Princess lifted her hips to urge DJ to fill her all the way up, and he did just that. He didn't stop until he was balls deep, and then he held it there as he sucked on her neck.

When he felt her warmth tighten around his hardness, he began to stroke in and out of her nice and slow at first, gradually picking up his pace until he could no longer restrain his wanting. Princess eagerly met his every hard thrust, loving the sweet pain and the taste of his sweat as it dripped onto her lips.

They made love until they fell asleep in each other's arms.

CHAPTER 23

DJ eased out of the bed in the dark and went into the bathroom as quietly as he could, trying not to wake Princess. He closed and locked the door behind him before turning on the lights.

"Meko?" Princess called, waking up in a mild panic after finding herself alone.

At the sound of her voice, DJ braced himself against the edge of the granite sink.

"I'm in the bathroom. I'll be right out!" he answered, looking at his reflection in the floral-framed mirror that he remembered trying to talk Lisa out of buying.

He was trying to see if he had changed into a monster like his mother told him he would if he did his woman wrong. It was his image looking back at him. He turned on the faucet and splashed cool water on his face.

Princess turned on the lamp next to the bed and propped herself up on her elbow. She wondered if the night was just a dream like all the others she had in the past. But the familiar soreness from the way only DJ could make her feel let her know that it was not. She wondered if it was the beer or if DJ really meant it when he said he still loved her and wanted her to stay. Princess wanted to believe him, but she had to be sure because of the way things had him acting. She still planned on sticking around for him because she couldn't run out on him again. She heard him flush and open the door. She finally got a good look at his ripped body as he walked back to bed and was ready for another round.

* * *

Show had spent the night in Meka's hospital room. She was asleep when he came in, so he didn't wake her. He had fallen asleep in the chair next to her bed trying to think of the best way to ask her to marry him. He had paid extra for the woman at Kay's to allow him to come inside and buy a ring after closing time. He didn't know what Meka would like, so he placed $10,000 on the counter and told the woman to give him something that would make her know he was for real.

"Show! Show?"

"Yeah, yeah! Hey, you!" he answered, returning the smile that Meka and the two nurses were giving him.

"Why you stalking me?" Meka asked jokingly.

"You get yourself into all types of bullshit if I don't!"

"Excuse me, but you have to step out so we can get her ready for the day."

"Get her ready for what?" he asked the nurse.

"I'm getting moved to Texas so they can fix me," Meka reminded him.

"I'm not leaving your side. I'm not leaving, so could you show me how to get her ready? I'ma need to know how to do this if I'm gonna take care of her on my own," Show said as he removed the diamond and ruby teardrop ring the saleswoman picked out for him.

"What the fuck is you doing? What you doing?" Meka asked again, tearing up right away.

"I'm asking you to let me love you for the rest of your life. I'm begging you to be my wife since you're already my life!" he told her while holding the ring out to her.

Show prayed she didn't say no in front of the two nurses.

"Yes, yes!"

She gave him her hand, and he placed the ring on her finger. She then pulled him into her, kissing him like she never had before.

"Y'all heard him. Please show this nigga what he needs to do before he wakes up!" Meka told the nurses while excitedly showing off the ring.

"Baby, just so you know, I already got your bro's blessing. I knew you would want me to. I thought I was gonna have to fight him for it," he told her with a grin.

"I wouldn't care if he said no. I'm the first one out, so that makes me the oldest," Meka joked, sounding just like her old self again.

EPILOGUE

Before Meka gave in to the powerful medication the general practitioner gave her, she kept telling herself she wasn't going to give up.

"If I can move my arms, I can move everything else," Meka whispered before she went into a deep sleep.

Meka woke up hours later in a recovery room.

"I'm alive!" she forced herself to choke out.

The room erupted with laughter. Show had not left her side as he promised her over and over on their flight down to Texas, but DJ and Princess arrived just a half hour before she awoke.

"Oh yeah, your ass is alive. I'm not gonna let you get away from me that easy!" Show told her.

"And I can't be a twin without my other half, punk!" DJ said as he walked over to the bed holding hands with Princess.

"Hey, girl!" Princess greeted her with tears of joy streaming down her cheeks.

"Why you crying? Why y'all holding hands like that?" Meka asked once she noticed.

"You know she's a cry baby, but you need to rest up. How you feeling, Meka?" DJ asked, now holding her hand.

"I'm cold and I'm tingling all over," she answered in a voice barely above a whisper. "I feel funny."

"Baby, that's good. The doc says it's gonna be that way for awhile, so don't worry," Show told her, trying to keep her from panicking.

"Will I be able to walk again?"

"You better or I'm just gonna have to roll your ass down to the pastor when we get married."

Meka's eyes brightened up when Show reminded her of their engagement.

"Where's my ring?" she demanded, holding up her hand to show it wasn't on her finger.

"I got it. They had to take it off when they put you under," Show explained as he pulled it out of his pocket.

"Put it back on so I can show it off!"

He did as she asked and kissed her dry lips.

"Hey, y'all can't be doing all that now! I can't believe you kissed them things. They look like sandpaper!" Princess teased her.

"Shut up, bitch, and come check out what my hubby gave me!"

"It's beautiful. I still can't believe your ass is getting married, bitch!" Princess said as she admired the ring on her best friend's finger.

Meka locked eves with her brother and saw the love she was feeling for Show in them and told him, "Don't trip. Your time's coming soon.

The End

Text Good2Go at 31996 to receive new release updates via text message.

To order books, please fill out the order form below:
To order films please go to www.good2gofilms.com

Name: __ _____

Address:_____

City: _____ State: _____ Zip Code: _____

Phone:_____

Email:_____

Method of Payment: Check   VISA   MASTERCARD

Credit Card#:_ _____

Name as it appears on card: _____

Signature: _____

Item Name	Price	Qty	Amount
48 Hours to Die – Silk White	$14.99		
A Hustler's Dream - Ernest Morris	$14.99		
A Hustler's Dream 2 - Ernest Morris	$14.99		
A Thug's Devotion – J. L. Rose and J. M. McMillon	$14.99		
Black Reign – Ernest Morris	$14.99		
Bloody Mayhem Down South – Trayvon Jackson	$14.99		
Bloody Mayhem Down South 2 – Trayvon Jackson	$14.99		
Business Is Business – Silk White	$14.99		
Business Is Business 2 – Silk White	$14.99		
Business Is Business 3 – Silk White	$14.99		
Childhood Sweethearts – Jacob Spears	$14.99		
Childhood Sweethearts 2 – Jacob Spears	$14.99		
Childhood Sweethearts 3 - Jacob Spears	$14.99		
Childhood Sweethearts 4 - Jacob Spears	$14.99		
Connected To The Plug – Dwan Marquis Williams	$14.99		
Connected To The Plug 2 - Dwan Marquis Williams	$14.99		
Connected To The Plug 3 – Dwan Marquis Williams	$14.99		
Connected To The Plug 4 – Dwan Marquis Williams	$14.99		
Deadly Reunion – Ernest Morris	$14.99		
Dream's Life – Assa Raymond Baker	$14.99		
Flipping Numbers – Ernest Morris	$14.99		
Flipping Numbers 2 – Ernest Morris	$14.99		
He Loves Me, He Loves You Not - Mychea	$14.99		
He Loves Me, He Loves You Not 2 - Mychea	$14.99		
He Loves Me, He Loves You Not 3 - Mychea	$14.99		
He Loves Me, He Loves You Not 4 – Mychea	$14.99		

He Loves Me, He Loves You Not 5 – Mychea	$14.99		
Lord of My Land – Jay Morrison	$14.99		
Lost and Turned Out – Ernest Morris	$14.99		
Married To Da Streets – Silk White	$14.99		
M.E.R.C. - Make Every Rep Count Health and Fitness	$14.99		
Money Make Me Cum – Ernest Morris	$14.99		
My Besties – Asia Hill	$14.99		
My Besties 2 – Asia Hill	$14.99		
My Besties 3 – Asia Hill	$14.99		
My Besties 4 – Asia Hill	$14.99		
My Boyfriend's Wife - Mychea	$14.99		
My Boyfriend's Wife 2 – Mychea	$14.99		
My Brothers Envy – J. L. Rose	$14.99		
My Brothers Envy 2 – J. L. Rose	$14.99		
Naughty Housewives – Ernest Morris	$14.99		
Naughty Housewives 2 – Ernest Morris	$14.99		
Naughty Housewives 3 – Ernest Morris	$14.99		
Naughty Housewives 4 – Ernest Morris	$14.99		
Never Be The Same – Silk White	$14.99		
Shades of Revenge – Assa Raymond Baker	$14.99		
Slumped – Jason Brent	$14.99		
Someone's Gonna Get It – Mychea	$14.99		
Stranded – Silk White	$14.99		
Supreme & Justice – Ernest Morris	$14.99		
Supreme & Justice 2 – Ernest Morris	$14.99		
Supreme & Justice 3 – Ernest Morris	$14.99		
Tears of a Hustler - Silk White	$14.99		
Tears of a Hustler 2 - Silk White	$14.99		
Tears of a Hustler 3 - Silk White	$14.99		
Tears of a Hustler 4- Silk White	$14.99		
Tears of a Hustler 5 – Silk White	$14.99		
Tears of a Hustler 6 – Silk White	$14.99		

The Panty Ripper - Reality Way	$14.99		
The Panty Ripper 3 – Reality Way	$14.99		
The Solution – Jay Morrison	$14.99		
The Teflon Queen – Silk White	$14.99		
The Teflon Queen 2 – Silk White	$14.99		
The Teflon Queen 3 – Silk White	$14.99		
The Teflon Queen 4 – Silk White	$14.99		
The Teflon Queen 5 – Silk White	$14.99		
The Teflon Queen 6 - Silk White	$14.99		
The Vacation – Silk White	$14.99		
Tied To A Boss - J.L. Rose	$14.99		
Tied To A Boss 2 - J.L. Rose	$14.99		
Tied To A Boss 3 - J.L. Rose	$14.99		
Tied To A Boss 4 - J.L. Rose	$14.99		
Tied To A Boss 5 - J.L. Rose	$14.99		
Time Is Money - Silk White	$14.99		
Tomorrow's Not Promised – Robert Torres	$14.99		
Tomorrow's Not Promised 2 – Robert Torres	$14.99		
Two Mask One Heart – Jacob Spears and Trayvon Jackson	$14.99		
Two Mask One Heart 2 – Jacob Spears and Trayvon Jackson	$14.99		
Two Mask One Heart 3 – Jacob Spears and Trayvon Jackson	$14.99		
Wrong Place Wrong Time – Silk White	$14.99		
Young Goonz – Reality Way	$14.99		
Subtotal:			
Tax:			
Shipping (Free) U.S. Media Mail:			
Total:			

Make Checks Payable To:
Good2Go Publishing
7311 W Glass Lane,
Laveen, AZ 85339

CPSIA information can be obtained
at www.ICGtesting.com
Printed in the USA
LVHW04s1532240918
591190LV00010B/814/P